"So this baby's father isn't going to be in the picture?" he said.

"That's right. I'm on my own."

And it won't be the first time. Liz didn't say the words. She didn't need to; her expression said it all.

"I want to talk about that," Matt said softly. "You shouldn't be standing around." He set his hand in the small of her back and steered her firmly across the foyer and into the sitting room. "I want you to rest on the patio, in the shade, while I make our dinner."

She came to a sudden halt. "I'm perfectly able to make my own din—"

He pressed a fingertip against her lips. "No slaving over a hot stove for you. Doctor's orders." Her full lips were soft and warm; he had to fight a sudden impulse to run his fingertip over the upper curve—

What happens when you suddenly discover your happy twosome is about to be turned into a...*family*?

Do you panic?
Do you laugh?
Do you cry?
Or...do you get married?

The answer is all of the above—and plenty more!

Share the laughter and the tears as these unsuspecting couples are plunged into parenthood! Whether it's a baby on the way, or the creation of a brand-new instant family, these men and women have no choice but to be

When parenthood takes you by surprise!

Look out in August 2001 for
The Bachelor's Baby
by Liz Fielding
#3666

TWINS INCLUDED!
Grace Green

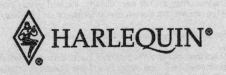

TORONTO • NEW YORK • LONDON
AMSTERDAM • PARIS • SYDNEY • HAMBURG
STOCKHOLM • ATHENS • TOKYO • MILAN • MADRID
PRAGUE • WARSAW • BUDAPEST • AUCKLAND

ISBN 0-373-03658-2

TWINS INCLUDED!

First North American Publication 2001.

CHAPTER ONE

"YOU'RE *pregnant?*"

Liz Rossiter felt a stab of apprehension as she saw angry crimson color mottle the face of the man seated across from her. "Yes, darling, I—"

"Dammit, Liz!" Colin Airdrie lurched forward in his chair and punched a fist down on the surface of their elegant Horrocks & Vine patio table. "You know I don't want any more kids. I've been there, done that. What the devil are you trying to do? *Trap* me?"

Déjà vu.

A fragment of memory—from the past that Liz had buried so carefully thirteen years before—suddenly broke free and surfaced, chilling her to the bone despite the sun beating down on their rooftop garden from a hazy New York sky.

This couldn't be happening.

Not now.

Not *again.*

"Colin," she said pleadingly, "it was an accident. I don't know how it happened." She tugged at her filigreed platinum choker, which all at once seemed to be strangling her. "But now that I *am* pregnant, I *want* this baby!"

Colin shoved back his chair and swung to his feet, his expression grim.

"Liz, I'm forty-five, as you well know. You also know that I have an ex-wife to support and three children to put through university—Amy's already there, the twins go next year. There's no *way* I want to start another family—''

''But…we *love* each other.''

''Right. And we've been in a committed relationship for more than five years. But you'll recall,'' he added tersely, ''that before we moved in together, we agreed that it would be just the two of us. And I haven't changed my mind. I don't want this baby. That's final.''

She stared at him, and it was like looking at a stranger. ''Surely,'' she whispered, ''surely you're not suggesting I should…should…''

She couldn't even bring herself to think it, far less say it. But she didn't need to. She could tell by the curt nod of his head that the unthinkable was exactly what he *was* suggesting.

''The choice is yours.'' Stepping behind his chair, he curled his fingers tightly around the top slat and fixed her with a hard implacable gaze. ''You can have either me or this child, Liz. You can't have both.''

Matthew Garvock flicked up his umbrella as he emerged from his Main Street law office in the small town of Tradition, British Columbia. Heavy rain had been pelting down all day and showed no signs of letting up.

He'd had a hectic week—and he rarely worked on Friday evenings but business was booming and he wasn't about to complain. The harder he worked, the more money he earned.

And it was money he could put to good use, he reflected as he strode along the rain-splashed sidewalk toward the brightly lit Pizza Palace in the next block.

The down payment for his new home had taken a huge chunk out of his savings—

A passing car suddenly veered too close to the gutter and sluiced muddy water in his direction. He jumped back, but it was too late. The damage was done. His pants were soaked, he could feel the fabric stick unpleasantly to his legs.

He glowered through the lashing rain and caught a glimpse of the offending vehicle just before it disappeared around the corner. It was a midnight-blue Porsche.

Didn't belong to anyone in town, he decided as he tugged sopping wet fabric from his knees before continuing on his way. Most folks in this neck of the woods drove pickup trucks. A Porsche was a city car—and this particular one had been driven by someone with city manners...which meant no manners.

He had occasion to visit Vancouver on business several times a year and was always glad to get home. People down on the Lower Mainland were all so damned busy going where they were going, they didn't care a *hoot* about anybody else.

He pressed his thumb against the top spring of his umbrella and shook the umbrella out as he walked into the Pizza Palace. It wasn't a place he regularly frequented—he didn't have to, Molly and his mother were forever bringing him casseroles or inviting him over for meals.

But tonight, because Molly had taken the kids to a movie, and his mother had gone to Kelowna for the weekend, he was on his own.

And he was looking forward to having the house to himself. Stressed-out after his hectic week, he needed some time alone. What he planned to do as soon as he got home was have a quick shower and change into dry clothes. Then he'd pour himself a beer and take it—along with a few slices of steaming Hawaiian pizza—through to the sitting room where he would spend a couple of mindless hours flaked out in front of the TV.

"Well, hallelujah, it's still here!"

Despite her aching fatigue and her screaming muscles, Liz managed a shaky smile as she dug up her old house key from among the clothes pegs stored in a wooden box by the back door of Laurel House.

Huddling under her hooded black slicker, she slipped the key into the lock, and held her breath. For a second, she met resistance...and then the dead bolt slid back.

Her breath seeped out in a relieved hiss and she slumped weakly against the door, heedless of the rain lashing down on her...

Then realizing she was in danger of falling asleep where she stood, she jerked herself upright. She had to stay awake...at least till she had faced her father.

She'd phoned him ten days ago, before setting off from New York, but he hadn't picked up the phone. She'd listened to his abrasive voice bark: "Max Rossiter here, leave a message after the beep!" but she hadn't wanted to leave a message. She had just wanted to confirm that he was still living in the family home.

Apparently he was...but this evening he was out.

She'd stood at the front door for a good five minutes, ringing the bell, over and over again. Finally she'd given up.

But she hadn't left.

On her long drive west, she'd had time to think.

And she had made some decisions. One of those decisions was that she was going to stand up to him. She wasn't going to let him intimidate her, the way he had when she was a teenager. Laurel House was his home...but it was also—legally—*her* home. And if he tried to throw her out, she would take him to court over it.

She opened the door and stepped inside.

Nothing had changed.

That was her first thought.

But after she'd taken a second look, she saw that some things had indeed changed. The appliances she remembered had been gold. The appliances she saw now were black. Gleaming black stove, dishwasher, fridge, microwave...

Yawning, she walked through the kitchen, out into the corridor and along to the foyer.

The doors to all the rooms were open, and she peeked in every one but they were all empty.

Yawning again, she turned away and ascended the stairs.

"Dad?" she called out as she reached the landing. Her voice echoed back. It had a hollow sound.

She checked his bedroom. He wasn't there. But everything was just as she remembered it, even to the blue-and-white antique quilt with its log cabin design.

She moved on to her old room. She was surprised but pleased to see that here, too, nothing had changed.

And never had the bed seemed more inviting.

Shrugging off her slicker, she tossed it over a chair. She would lie down, she decided exhaustedly, and have a short nap. But she'd leave the door open to make sure that when her father came home, she would hear him.

* * *

She woke from a deep sleep to the sound of movement. The thud of heavy footsteps, someone going down the stairs.

She pushed herself up to a sitting position, and felt her fingers tremble as she brushed her long sleep-mussed hair back. Her father was home. And she had to go down and face him. It was a moment she'd dreaded.

She edged off the bed and crept to the door. And hesitated.

The courage she'd built up during her journey now threatened to desert her. Her father's rages...they had always *terrified* her.

But she had to confront him sometime. And what was to be gained by putting it off?

Swallowing down her dread, she made her decision. And before she could change her mind, she walked out of her room, across the landing and then—forcing one foot after the other—she descended the stairs.

Matt had just gulped a mouthful of beer from his can when he heard a sound behind him.

Swiveling around, he spluttered when he saw the pale apparition standing unsteadily in the doorway—a wraithlike figure with long flaxen hair and a perfect oval face.

"What the...?" Wondering if he was dreaming, he stared incredulously. Then shaking his head vehemently, he tried to jar the vision from his head. But...when he looked again, it was still there. *She* was still there.

And she was staring at him as incredulously as if he, too, were a ghost. Her eyes were starkly wide, her full lips parted in dismay, her oval face as pale as the crumpled ecru suit that hung so loosely on her thin body.

"There must," he said, "be some explanation for this. Tell me——" he attempted to inject some humor into his tone "——please tell me that you're not the Phantom Lady of Laurel House!"

"What," she asked in a voice as insubstantial as her appearance, "are *you* doing here?"

She was real. No doubt about it. Ghosts didn't wear perfume and this one was wearing something that made him think of pink roses and summer kisses. Raising his beer can to his mouth again, he regarded her with great interest as he took another long swig.

Then wiping the froth from his lips, he set the can on the counter and settled his fists lightly on his hips.

"I'm here," he said in an amused tone, "because this is my home."

Her eyes, if that were possible, widened even further. "Since when?" One of her hands had crept to her throat and she was pulling her delicately fashioned platinum choker from her neck as if trying to keep it from strangling her.

Who the devil was she? And what did she want?

"Since when?" she demanded.

"Since I bought it."

"You've *bought* it? Bought Laurel House? But you can't have! What happened to——"

"The previous owner? Max Rossiter?" He shrugged. "He'd been ill for a long time and he passed away a couple of months ago——"

She made an odd sound, like the croak of a parched frog.

Intrigued by her reaction, he kept talking and watched her with fast-growing curiosity. "Shortly before that, he'd put the house up for sale—it's only two miles out of town and it has the greatest view, so I bought it. It had been mortgaged to the hilt—the old guy had had a stroke several years back and he just couldn't keep up with his extra expenses so in the end he was forced to sell..."

If she'd been pale before, she was ashen now. Alarmingly so.

He walked over to her. "You need to sit down." He reached out a hand to take her arm in support, but she tried to twist away and his fingertips accidentally brushed her breasts before he cupped her elbow. "You look all in—"

She wrenched herself free and stumbled back. "Don't touch me!" She glared at him. "Don't you dare touch me!"

Stunned by her hostility, he stepped back, his palms up. "Whoa, hold on, lady. You've got the wrong idea. I'm not looking to *ravish* you."

Her eyes had become icy cold, but her cheeks were fiery red. "If you were, Matthew Garvock, it wouldn't be the first time."

Jolted more by the bitterness of her tone than the fact that she knew his name, he gaped at her. Had they met somewhere before? If so, he had no memory of it. He tried to see beyond the pale skin and the pale hair and the pale clothes, to the person vibrating with such blatant antagonism behind them.

And finally, just as he was about to give up, he recognized her.

"Good Lord." He felt his heart tremble. "It's Beth." Emotion threatened to close his throat. "I can't believe you've come back. After all this time."

She had regained her composure. And she fixed him with a gaze so stony it tore him apart.

"Yes, it's me, Matt. I'm back…and I'm here to stay. As to Laurel House being your 'home'—"

At last he'd found his voice again. "You're welcome to stay here, for as long as you want—"

Her laugh was harsh. "Oh, I plan to. You see, Matt, this is rightfully *my* home, despite what my father may have led you and his lawyer to believe—"

He was hardly listening to her. He could scarcely believe she'd come back after all these years. Thirteen years. Thirteen years during which he'd never managed to shake free of the racking guilt and the aching regrets—

"…so tomorrow," she was saying, "I'll go see Judd Anstruther, my father's lawyer, and I'll sort everything out."

With an effort, he focused on what she was saying.

"Judd's retired," he said.

"Who took over his practice?"

"I did. Whatever you decide to do, I'll be involved." Agitatedly he raked a hand through his shower-damp hair. "Beth, we have to talk. About…what happened, thirteen years ago—"

"No." Her throat rippled convulsively. "You have *nothing* to say to me that I would want to listen to. But I have two things to say to you. And I want *you* to listen, because I don't want to say them twice. The first is, don't call me Beth. I'm no longer that naive teenager, and I no longer go by that name. If you have to call me anything, call me Liz. Or Ms. Rossiter. Either will do and I answer to both…but in your case, I'd prefer the latter."

He had slipped the pizza into the oven to keep it

warm while he had his shower; now he noticed the steamy smell of pepperoni and grilled cheese, and he knew he would always associate that specific aroma with this specific moment.

"And the second thing?" he asked.

The faint lines bracketing her mouth deepened. "Don't *ever*," she said, "try to talk to me about the past."

Uh-uh. No way. He wasn't about to go along with that. "But I want to t—"

"You want to what? To say you're *sorry?*"

"I want you to know that afterward I tried to—"

"*Afterward?*" Her mocking tone made him wince. "Matthew, I have absolutely *no* interest in what happened *afterward.*"

"But—"

She stopped him by slashing a hand between them. "But what?" she asked fiercely. "Do you have anything to say that can change what happened? Can you change the past?"

She had broken his heart when she'd disappeared out of his life. But he knew he must have broken her heart, too. And while he had deserved all the agony he'd suffered, she had not.

"No," he said wearily. "No, I can't."

"Then please don't try." Her tone was crisp. "And please don't ever bring up the subject again. I've put the past behind me. And you," she said as she turned away, and started toward the door, "would be wise to do the same."

He moved fast and got to the door before she did. Blocking her exit, he said, "Where are you going?"

"To bed."

"I'm not budging from the house. I paid good money for it. And I have all the papers to prove it."

As soon as he'd spoken, he felt like a heel. Now that he was close to her, he realized she was even more fragile than she'd seemed. Fragile and vulnerable.

And here he was, confronting her, in the way a school bully would challenge a weaker child. Remorse poured through him like bile.

"So what are we going to do now?" he asked gruffly. "It looks as if we've reached an impasse."

Fragile and vulnerable she might be, and bone-tired by the looks of her, but she was one thing, he saw as she straightened her spine, that she hadn't been as a teenager.

Liz Rossiter was a fighter.

She looked up at him, and in her beautiful khaki eyes he could have sworn he saw a spark of cynical humor.

"You're bigger than I am," she said, "and as I recall you were a champion amateur boxer, so I won't even try to throw you out. At least, not bodily. But you'd better start looking for another place to stay, because I promise you, Matthew Garvock, I'm going to win back this house."

"Is that," he asked softly, "a declaration of war?"

"Oh, yes," she said, in a tone that was equally soft—as soft as steel, he thought, sheathed in a velvet glove!—"a declaration of war is *exactly* what it is!"

CHAPTER TWO

LIZ slept badly.

Her father had been a difficult man to love but still her pillow had been drenched with the tears she had shed for him before she finally drifted off. Then her dreams had been racked by images of him in one of his rages, so that when she woke up in the morning, it was with a feeling of guilty relief that she would never have to face him again.

Later, as she stood under the hot spray of the shower, her thoughts slid inexorably to Matt.

She'd been stunned to find him in the kitchen—although of course she hadn't at first recognized him. At some time during the thirteen years she'd been away, someone had—to put it politely!—rearranged his face.

The Matt she remembered had been attractive in a clean-cut way, his lean features symmetrically sculpted and his face unscarred despite his many bouts as an amateur boxer.

"Pretty Boy." That's what his university buddies had called him, and he'd accepted the nickname with good humor. But he'd confided to Liz that keeping his face unmarked was a point of honor with him. As a fifteen-year-old, he'd promised his concerned mother that if she gave him permission to join the school boxing club, he'd never hurt her by coming home with his face battered. He'd kept that promise.

At least while Liz knew him. But now...no one

would ever call him Pretty Boy again. His hair was the same—black with copper highlights; his eyes still dark-lashed and the incredibly rich green of a glacial lake. But his nose had been broken and was markedly ridged; one cheekbone had been flattened; and his lower lip sported a thin, long scar.

He looked tough now, and he looked rugged.

And he still—heaven help her!—made her heart beat faster.

But he must never know it.

And he must never know that she'd lied when she said she never thought about the past. Now that she was pregnant again, she thought about it all the time. Thought about him, and the sweet love they had shared, and the child they had so passionately, yet so tenderly, created together.

Stepping out of the shower, she reached for a towel and swiped it over the mirror. She stared at herself, her reflection shimmering in the wet glass. It was no wonder, she mused ironically, that he hadn't recognized her. She barely recognized herself, she looked so colorless. The girl he knew had been vibrant and pretty, with bouncy blond curls and a healthy pink glow in her cheeks.

She sighed as she blow-dried her hair. She and Matt had both changed. And they would never again be the same. They were different people now, with different lives.

And though Tradition was a small town, it was big enough for both of them. It would *have* to be, she decided resolutely, because she had no intention of leaving.

And once she'd ousted him from Laurel House, she would burrow in and make it her home. A warm and comfortable home, for herself and her new baby...the baby that was now the only important thing in her life.

"You, Ms. Rossiter, are one very careless driver!"

Seated alone at the kitchen table, Liz was startled by the sound of Matt's voice as he came in through the back door. She jumped, and almost spilled her coffee.

Putting down the mug, she dropped her hands to her lap, and hoped she looked calmer than she felt. She wasn't used to this new Matt—wasn't used to the hard, craggy face, wasn't used to the maturity of his bearing.

In the moments before he shut the door, a draft of morning air swept into the room, making her shiver. Or had she shivered because his powerful tanned body was so blatantly revealed in jogging shorts and a black tank top?

"Careless? Really?" She kept her tone casual. And not unfriendly. "Why would you think that?"

A wary expression flickered in his eyes, causing her nervousness to dissipate in a surge of satisfaction. Her amicable attitude had thrown him off balance...and she liked the feeling of control!

He scowled at her. "The Porsche parked out back is yours?"

She nodded, and quirked a quizzical eyebrow.

"Then you owe me."

"For what?"

"For splashing mud over my suit," he growled. "Last night, on Main Street—"

"Oh, that was *you!*"

"You *knew* you'd soaked me?" Indignation resonated in his husky voice. "But you didn't stop to apologize?"

"Sorry. I knew I'd splashed somebody...and if I'd known it was a *lawyer*..." She chuckled. "So...sue me!"

His scowl deepened. Before he could say anything, she added contritely, "Look, I really am sorry. But truly I couldn't help it. A cat darted in front of the car and I had to swerve to avoid it. If I'd had time to think," she added, dead-pan, "I would of course have chosen to kill the cat rather than splatter your suit. I mean, let's get our priorities straight here. What is it, by the way...just as a matter of interest? An Armani? A Canali?"

He glared at her for a further moment...and then his laughter rolled out, free and easy as an eagle on the wing.

"Sears," he said. "Off-the-rack."

She leaned back in her chair, her expression mocking. "Whatever happened," she asked, "to the teenager who swore that when he graduated from law school, he'd never buy off-the-rack clothes again?"

"What happened," he retorted, "was that he found much better ways to spend his money. Besides—" he threw her a lazy smile that curled her toes "—most of my clients are from the local farming community. They come into my office in their working clothes— oftimes reeking of manure, if not trailing it in on their boots!—and we all feel more comfortable if I'm not dressed up like some city slicker."

"But yesterday—"

"Yesterday I had to go to court with a client, but normally I wear jeans to the office." He wiped a forearm over his brow, leaving a glaze of sweat. "So...did you sleep well?"

"Yes," she fibbed. "I did. I'd been on the road for

over a week and I was bushed. Besides, there's nothing to beat sleeping in one's own bed.''

A green-and-white striped hand towel dangled from a hook on the wall by the door. Reaching for it, he said in a teasing voice, ''You think?''

She felt her cheeks grow warm. The last thing she wanted was to get in a conversation with this man about sleeping in any bed other than her own. ''Yes.''

''Ah, well,'' he drawled, ''to each his...or her... own.'' He rubbed the towel over his damp hair and then ran it over his neck and arms. Slinging it back on the hook, he glanced at the carafe of coffee she'd made earlier. ''Can I have some of that?'' Without waiting for an answer, he poured himself a mug, and pulling out the chair across from her, he sat down.

''So,'' he said, ''you'd been on the road for over a week. Where'd you come from?''

''New York.''

''Ah, a city gal. So, city gal, how about filling me in on what you've been doing the past thirteen years. That's one expensive vehicle you're running. You must either have a good job...or you married into money.''

''Neither,'' she said. ''I don't have a job and I don't have a husband.''

Silence swelled between them, broken only by the hum of the refrigerator. He was the first to speak.

''You're on your own?''

She hesitated. Eventually he—and everybody else in Tradition—would learn that she was pregnant. But for the time being, she wanted to keep that secret to herself.

''Yes,'' she said. Then, to divert him, she said, ''I

want to go and visit my father's grave. Is he at Fairlawn?''

"No, they built a new cemetery ten years ago—it's out past Miller's Farm, take the second road on your left...or is it the third?'' He scratched a hand through his tousled hair. "I know how to get there but—tell you what, I'll drive you—''

"Thanks, I'd like to drive myself. I'll buy a map.''

"You didn't use to be so independent!''

He'd said it without thinking, but when he saw a shadow darken her eyes, he could have kicked himself. If she was independent now, it was because she'd had to be. When she'd most needed support, when she had most *desperately* needed support, she'd been let down by those she should have been able to depend on the most.

She pushed back her chair and got to her feet. "I am independent, Matt.'' She spoke quietly. "And I *cherish* my independence. I've learned the hard way that the only person I can count on is myself.''

He stood, too, and fisting his hands by his sides, faced her steadily across the table. "You're wrong, Beth. If there's ever anything I can do for you, just say the word.''

She looked at him, for the longest time. And then she said, with a twisted little half smile. "There *is* one thing you can do for me, Matt.''

"Sure.'' His heart leaped in anticipation. "What?''

"Please,'' she said, "*don't* call me 'Beth.'''

And without another word, she flicked back her long flaxen hair and stalked regally out of the kitchen.

Liz bought a recently published map of the area, in the London Drugs on Jefferson Street.

She asked the obliging clerk to mark the position of the new cemetery, and fifteen minutes after leaving the store, she was pulling the Porsche up in the carpark of the Greenvale Burial Grounds.

"Way to go, kid!"

"Thanks, Uncle Matt!"

"Well done, Stuart." Molly Martin gave her breathless eight-year-old son a warm hug. "That was a great game and you were a star!"

"Where's Iain?" Stuart whipped off his baseball cap and sent a searching look around for his younger brother.

"He's gone to book us one of the picnic tables." Matt popped open the can of lemonade he was holding, and gave it to the flushed youngster. "You ready for lunch?"

"Am I ever!"

"Then let's get this show on the road."

As the threesome made their way from the baseball field to the adjoining park, Stuart ran on ahead while Molly tucked her arm through Matt's.

"Too bad you couldn't have come to that movie with us last night," she said. "You'd really have enjoyed it."

"Yeah. But I didn't get out of the office till after seven. I don't remember when I was ever quite so busy."

They stopped by Matt's dusty black Taurus, which he'd left in the carpark adjacent to the street, and he hefted his picnic cooler from the trunk. Molly slammed the lid.

"I hope," she said as they headed into the park, "that you took time to eat dinner."

"I took home a pizza."

"There's lots of nourishment in a good pizza."

"I guess."

What he didn't tell her was that he hadn't eaten one crumb of the takeout pizza. By the time he and Beth— he and *Liz!*—had finished talking—had finished *arguing!*—the last thing on his mind had been food.

Frowning, he mulled over his present situation.

He knew he had to tell Molly that Max Rossiter's daughter had turned up and had moved back into her old home.

His home, now.

Although she was, apparently, determined to battle him for it.

He hadn't found quite the right moment to tell Molly of this new development; and he wasn't sure he knew *why* he was so reluctant to bring it up.

"Hey, Mom, over here!" Iain waved to them from a picnic table. "Let's get that cooler open, I'm starving!"

"Hold your horses, young man!" Matt placed the cooler on the table, and the two boys immediately set themselves to unlatching the lid.

Matt helped Molly to her seat, but as he sat down beside her, his eyes were on the two brown-haired boys kneeling on the bench at the other side of the table as they eagerly unpacked the food and set it out.

He'd made a point of spending as much time as he could with them after they lost their dad. And with Molly, too. Unknown to Molly, before Dave died he'd asked Matt to take care of her after he'd gone. And that promise, made to his longtime best friend, was sacred to Matt.

"You seem a bit distracted," Molly said. "Is something wrong?"

"Sorry. My mind just wandered for a bit. Everything's fine." He made an effort to concentrate, and kept up his part in the conversation during their lunch.

After they were finished, they packed up, and the boys ran over to a set of swings by the nearby tennis courts.

He and Molly walked back to the car, and as he put the cooler in the trunk, she said,

"I'm going to pop over to the washrooms. Be right back."

Matt strolled over to the swings. Leaning against one of the uprights, he smiled as he watched the boys fly high.

After a couple of minutes, they jumped off, and they all three walked back to the Taurus.

As the boys got in, Matt saw Molly come running toward him, the sun dancing in her brown hair.

She'd had it cut last week.

"Very short," she'd told him that evening, over the phone. "For the summer!" And short it was. But it suited her dainty features, and emphasized her large hazel eyes.

She'd lost a lot of weight in the months following Dave's death, but now he noticed how nicely she was filling out her T-shirt again, and how attractively her denim skirt lay over her trim hips.

When she came to a breathless stop beside him, he smiled. "You've put on a bit of weight. It suits you."

"If I keep eating the way I've been doing lately, I'll soon be 'deliciously plump' again!"

Matt laughed with her as they recalled the teasing

words Dave had always used to describe his wife's curves.

"Yeah," he said. "Dave would be pleased."

"You know, Matt, if someone had told me, just after Dave was killed, that one day I'd be laughing again, I wouldn't have believed them. But now…"

"Yeah. Time heals. I guess it's really true."

She put a hand on his arm and looked up at him. "I don't know if I'd have survived, if it hadn't been for you."

"It works both ways, sweetie. I've missed Dave, too." He put an arm around her, and as he embraced her, he inhaled her floral scent, which was as familiar to him now as the feel of her soft body in his arms. He had comforted her—as she had comforted him— so many times…but never in any sexual way. Nor was there anything sexual in their embrace now.

"Come on, you guys!" Stuart said. "Iain's gonna be late for his chess lesson!"

Once Matt had settled Molly in the car, he walked around to his own side, but before he opened his door, he heard a car idling in the street and got the feeling that someone was watching him.

He glanced across and saw that the vehicle with the idling engine was hovering at the far side of the road.

It was a midnight-blue Porsche. The driver was Liz.

Their eyes met. Her expression was startled.

And that was all he had time to see before she rammed her foot down on the accelerator and raced away.

Liz's thoughts were in turmoil as she drove home.

She could have *kicked* herself for pausing at the park. She'd been passing by it and when she'd

chanced to see Matt stroll from his car, alone, she
had—on an impulse—slowed her own car down.

It had occurred to her that she might join him. She
had some questions she wanted to ask him, about her
father. Then he'd started chatting with a couple of
boys who'd been playing on the swings.

She decided to wait till he was alone again, but all
three walked over to his car. Then a woman ran up.
It was immediately obvious that she was with Matt.
And when Matt took her in his arms and held her
close, it was just as obvious that they were in a relationship.

Knowing she should move on but unable to drag
her gaze away, Liz had felt a heavy ache in her heart.
She had assumed that Matt lived alone. Well, perhaps
he lived alone...but he wasn't unattached.

She herself wanted nothing to do with him...yet
why did seeing him with someone else upset her so?

She'd been about to drive on when he'd spotted her.

Their eyes had locked, and even from the distance
she had seen the surprise in his. What had he seen in
hers? she wondered. She only hoped he hadn't seen
her distress.

It was going to be intolerable living at Laurel House
with him. Even if he and the stranger weren't actually
cohabiting, she would surely be a frequent visitor.

And Liz knew she couldn't bear to see them together. Just the sight of him with another woman in
his arms had torn every old scar off her heart. And
she knew, with a sinking feeling of despair, that even
after all these years, Matt Garvock still had the power
to hurt her.

*   *   *

He didn't come home that night till well after nine.

Liz was upstairs in the small room which had been her study as a teenager. She'd spent the evening sorting old correspondence and school papers, tossing out most of it, saving only items that had special meaning for her. The task had kept her busy; had kept her from thinking about Matt, and she'd succeeded...till she tugged the faded liner from the bottom drawer and found a scrap of paper that had been tucked underneath.

On the scrap she saw the words she'd printed there the day she'd realized she was pregnant with Matt's baby:

Beth Garvock
   Mrs. Matthew Garvock
   Mr. and Mrs. Matt Garvock

As she looked at the words now, a torrent of memories brought tears to her eyes. She'd been so naively trusting, so sure Matt would ask her to marry him...

Instead he'd let her down badly.

But his failure to stand by her hadn't dimmed the joy and wonder she'd felt at the prospect of being a mother.

And this time around, her wonder and her joy were just as intense.

Sometimes, though, she worried in case anything went wrong with her pregnancy. And sometimes she felt totally overwhelmed by the responsibility of being a single mom.

But over and above her anxieties was an unwavering determination to be the best parent she could possibly be...in a way that her own father had never been for her. More than *anything,* a baby needed love. And she already loved this child more than words could express—

A light double tap on the door made her jump. Automatically she crushed the scrap of paper into a ball and threw it into the garbage pail where it got lost in a jumble of scribblers and *Teen* magazines and exam papers.

"Liz?" Matt's voice was tired. "May I come in?"

She sat frozen, not answering, her heart thudding wildly.

"Liz?" This time his voice had a hard edge. "I need to talk to you. I'm coming in now."

CHAPTER THREE

MATT pushed the door open.

And saw Liz scrambling up from her chair.

She stood facing him, leaning back against the edge of the desk. She seemed actually to be trying to press into it, as if desperate to get away from him.

"You can't come bursting in here anytime you want," she said. "Please respect my right to some privacy."

"Liz." He moved forward but stopped a few feet from her when he met the wall of hostility she'd erected between them. With a pleading gesture, he said, "I'm not your enemy. You seem to think of me as some kind of a threat—"

"You're wrong, Matt. I don't think of you at all."

He sighed. This conversation was going nowhere. Or at least, it wasn't going in the direction he wanted it to.

He started again. "All I wanted to ask was...did you find the cemetery?"

"Yes."

"And your father's grave?"

"Yes."

"I know," he said, "that you and your dad never got along...but still, it must have been tough."

To his dismay, he saw a mist of tears in her eyes. Tears which she quickly blinked away.

"What was tough," she said levelly, "was finding out from the caretaker that in the weeks before he died,

29

my father was...incarcerated—for want of a better word!—in Blackwells Nursing Home.''

"Incarcerated...that's kind of harsh, Liz."

"Harsh? I don't think so! That place, as I recall, was like something out of a Dickens' novel. The only people who ended up at Blackwells were people who couldn't afford anything better. So tell me, has it changed?" she demanded.

"No, it hasn't."

"I don't understand how my father ended up there then. He had *pots* of money."

"Most of it was apparently invested in the stock market and a few years after you left, he lost it. It was the news of that loss that brought on his stroke."

She swallowed hard, and her voice shook a little as she asked, "How did he cope...after the stroke?"

He knew she was finding this conversation difficult, but there was no way he could make it any easier for her. The facts were the facts, and he wouldn't be doing her any favors by sugarcoating them. If she didn't hear them from him, she would hear them from someone else. "He had to have a round-the-clock attendant."

"Where did he get the money for that?"

"It was a costly business and as I mentioned before, that's why he eventually had to mortgage the house. In the end, just before he went into Blackwells, he had to put the place up for sale to pay his debts. The day before I put in my offer, he had another stroke. And then a few weeks later, he had his fatal heart attack..."

"How sad to end up like that. With no family around, and in a place like Blackwells. I should have come home years ago." Liz hid her face in her hands and started to sob, muffled little sounds seeping out between her fingers.

He couldn't bear to see her so distressed.

With a groan, he closed the space between them and drew her tenderly into his arms. "I knew this would be tough for you," he murmured. "That's why I wanted to drive you to the cemetery. But you didn't want me around. You wanted no part of me."

She felt so fragile he was afraid she might snap in his embrace. Like the most delicate of crystal. Anguish twisted his heart. She had once been his, and through a moment of stupidity and immaturity, he had lost her.

He looked down at her as she leaned against him, weeping gently.

And he felt a ray of hope.

She'd wasted no time last night in telling him she was independent, but...was she *really* so independent? She wasn't fighting him now, *was* she? Maybe this was the time to press his case again. He so desperately wanted the opportunity to make amends.

"Liz, please let me help you," he begged. "I'd do anything to—"

She jerked away from him, and with a little hiccuping sob, glared at him through eyes that shone with tears.

"I don't *need* help." She dashed a hand over her eyes. "And if I did, you'd be the last person in the world I'd turn to. I can handle this on my own!"

She was a fighter. Once again, the word came into his mind. Liz Rossiter was no longer the easily intimidated girl she'd been at seventeen; she was strong and she was determined.

And she *didn't* need him in her life. He was going to have to accept that; but it wasn't going to be easy.

"Just tell me one more thing," she said. "About this house."

"Anything."

"My father was under great pressure to sell."

"Yeah, he was—"

"So you got yourself a good deal? I mean, if he was under pressure—"

"I'm not sure what you're implying, Liz." But he knew damned well what she implying. She was implying that he had taken advantage of an old man's desperate financial plight; whereas, in actual fact, he'd had to stretch himself to the limit to come up with the asking price.

"So tell me," she said, with a careless shrug of one shoulder, "were you happy with the deal you made?"

He somehow managed to hide the anger he felt at her insinuating tone. "Happy?" He lifted one shoulder, mimicking her careless shrug. "I wouldn't have used the word 'happy.' But I was certainly more than satisfied."

"I'll bet!" Her scorn was blatant. And it didn't sit prettily on her face.

He wanted to wipe that contemptuous expression away, he burned to tell her exactly why he had bought Laurel House, but his pride wouldn't let him.

And what did it matter anyway? He could never redeem himself, in her eyes, for the wrong he'd done her thirteen years ago. He could live with her believing he had screwed her father. He'd lived with worse.

"Okay." He rubbed a hand wearily over his jaw. "I'll let you get back to whatever you were doing."

He left her standing there, and he didn't look back.

Next day was sunny and very warm, and Liz decided to attend the eleven o'clock service at the Presbyterian Church.

But when she tried to start the car she found she had carelessly let it run out of gas.

Even if she'd wanted to—which she didn't!—she couldn't have asked Matt for a drive as she'd heard him leave the house an hour before. So she took off at a brisk pace and walked the couple of miles into town.

By the time she got to the church, it was five after eleven. As she ran up the steps and across the deserted narthex, she could hear the congregation singing.

The music faded to an end as she pushed open the swing doors, and in the bustle of movement as everyone sat down, she slipped unnoticed into one of the back pews.

"Matt, will you pop down to the basement and pick up the boys from Sunday School?" Molly adjusted the brim of her straw hat as she looked up at Matt. They were standing in the narthex, jostled together by the jovial crowd making its way out to the street on this lovely sunny Sunday.

"You're not coming down?"

"No, I need to dash home...the service was longer than usual and I want to check on the roast. Will you pick up the boys and take them to my place?"

"Sure, no problem. But Molly—"

"Mmm?" She was impatient as a horse at the starting gate. "What is it, Matt? I really *must* dash."

"Okay, honey. Go ahead. But—" he rested his hand lightly on her shoulder "—I need to have a talk with you. Today."

Her hazel eyes took on a luminous glow. "The boys have been invited over to Jamie's after lunch. We'll be on our own and we can talk privately." She ran a hand down his striped silk tie. And let her fingertips linger for a moment. "Hurry home, Matt. I'll be waiting."

Liz walked along Fourth Avenue, the echo of her steps a rather lonely sound on the Sunday-quiet street.

She'd slipped away as the congregation sang the last hymn. She knew she'd have to face everyone eventually, but she'd decided to put it off till another day. She still felt drained after her visit to the cemetery; and her confrontation with Matt last night hadn't helped.

Nor had it helped when he'd pulled her into his arms.

For a moment—only a moment though it had seemed like an eternity—she'd allowed herself the luxury of leaning on him. But when he'd offered, in that husky sexy voice, to help her, to do anything—

His words had jerked her back to reality as surely as if he'd slapped her face.

She could not depend on this man. And she must never forget it.

Picking up her step, she was almost at the corner of the block, when a sudden squeal of tires grabbed her attention. A white Honda Civic had braked in the road just ahead...and was backing up toward her.

When it stopped, she saw that the driver was a woman—a stranger wearing a floral dress, a wide-brimmed straw hat and sunglasses that hid her eyes.

"Beth?" The car window was open, the woman's tone high with astonishment. "Beth Rossiter? Is it really you?"

Liz frowned. "I'm sorry," she murmured, walking over to the car. "I don't—"

The stranger's laugh gurgled out. "Oh, Beth. It's me!" She whisked off her hat and her sunglasses and tossed them onto the passenger seat. "There, is that better?" She ruffled a hand through her short brown hair and poked her head out the window. "Recognize me now?"

It was Molly White. Liz felt a surge of delight. She and Molly had been buddies all the way up through school until they were fourteen, at which time Molly's father—a policeman—had been transferred to Vancouver and the family had moved away. She and Molly had lost touch after that.

"Molly!" Leaning over, she brushed a kiss over her friend's warm cheek, and smelled her light floral fragrance. "It's *wonderful* to see you again. When did you come back to Tradition? And how have you been, what are you doing now?"

"It's a long story and I'd love for us to get together and catch up on each other's news but I don't have time right now. I'm on my way home to rescue a roast from the oven. I'm making a special lunch for my crew."

"Your crew?"

"I'm a widow, with two little boys. And—" Molly's cheeks colored prettily "—there's a man in my life—you wouldn't know him, he was three years ahead of us in high school." She didn't wait for Liz to respond, but just barreled on. "Anyway, he and I have been seeing each other for a while now and we have an…understanding. And before very long, I expect—" She broke off with a vexed "Tsk!" And gushed on, "Oh, I shouldn't have said that! Matt—Matt Garvock, that's his name—prob'ly wouldn't

want me to be talking about it. Not yet. You won't
say anything to a soul, will you?''

Liz hoped she didn't look as numb as she felt.
''No,'' she somehow managed to say, ''I won't say a
word.'' Molly and Matt. Molly was the woman he'd
been with in the park, though Liz hadn't recognized
her at the time.

''Thanks, I really appreciate it!'' Molly set the
Honda in motion again, and as she pulled away she
called back merrily, ''Give me a call, Beth, my number's in the book. It's under my married name...
Martin. Molly Martin. We'll have coffee together
soon...and by then I should have some lovely news
to share with you!''

Matt took off his suit jacket and slung it over one of
the Adirondack chairs arranged on Molly's front veranda. Then tugging open the top button of his dress
shirt, he loosened the knot of his tie as he followed
the boys into the house.

Iain and Stuart ran upstairs to change out of their
best clothes, and Matt went looking for Molly.

He followed the aroma of roasting beef and found
her in the kitchen, pouring gravy into a gravy boat.

''Hi,'' he said. ''We're back.''

She turned, and he saw that her face was flushed
from the heat of the oven. She set the gravy boat on
the table, and said, ''You'll never *guess* what happened on my way home!''

''You got a ticket for speeding?'' he teased.

''If I did, it would be a first! No, Matt. I was driving
along Fourth when I spotted a friend I hadn't seen
in...oh, must be close to sixteen years! She'd changed
a bit...but I knew her by the way she walked...that

hadn't changed. And her legs, of course! Beth Rossiter always did have the most fabulous legs. In high school, we were all pea-green with envy! Anyway,'' she said, beaming at him, ''you'll meet her soon because—''

''I've met her, Molly.''

Molly did a double take. ''You *have?* But... where?''

He should have told her yesterday and he could kick himself now that he hadn't. It wasn't as if there hadn't been plenty opportunity. They'd been together all day—first at the baseball game, then after Iain's chess lesson he'd driven them all the fifty miles to Crestville for the Farmers' Fair, and they hadn't got back till late evening.

''Matt? Do you *know* Beth Rossiter?''

''Honey, that's what I wanted to talk to you about.''

Her brow wrinkled, and she looked at him as if she didn't quite understand what he'd said.

''At the church,'' he reminded her. ''When I told you I needed to talk to you? It was about—''

''About Beth?''

He couldn't understand why she suddenly looked so disappointed. What had she thought he wanted to discuss with her?

''Liz,'' he said. ''She goes by the name of Liz now. She turned up at Laurel House on Friday night. She didn't know her father had died...didn't know he'd sold the family home.''

''Oh, my! What a dreadful shock she must have had when you told her—although, as I recall, she and her father didn't get along at all well. He was a frightful man, prone to the most awful rages. So...is she here on holiday? And where is she staying? Did she book in at Sandford's Inn?''

"I believe the move's permanent. And no, she's not booked in at Sandford's. She's staying at the house."

"You surely don't mean Laurel House?''

"Yeah," he said. "She's there. With me. For the present, at any rate, till we sort things out."

"But…what things?''

"She says she has papers that prove her father had no right to sell the property—''

"But everything was legal, wasn't it? I mean, you're a lawyer, for heaven's sake! You'd have checked everything out—''

"Oh, it's legal all right. No question about that.''

"Then…she'll have to leave. Find another place to stay. Won't she?''

"It's not all that simple, Molly—''

Matt broke off as he heard the boys clattering downstairs.

He put a hand on Molly's shoulder.

"Let's leave it for now," he said quietly. "We'll talk some more, after lunch.''

Liz had always loved Laurel House.

She knew it was partly because the rambling old place had such character, but it was also because of the memories it held of her mother, and the love they had shared until her mother's death when Liz was twelve.

Now on this Sunday afternoon, knowing Matt wouldn't be back for a while, Liz was free to roam around the place at will—not that she wanted to poke around among *his* things; she just wanted to reacquaint herself with her old home.

On the night of her arrival, she'd noticed the new appliances in the kitchen; and in the morning, she'd seen that the cupboards were new, too. But apart from that, everything seemed much as she remembered. And on her tour of the main floor, she found little had changed there, either. Even the furniture was the same. Matt's deal with her father must have included the contents of the house.

A deal which, she had already decided cynically, had probably been very sweet indeed. For Matt.

Upstairs, she found the first of the two guest rooms had obviously been taken over by the new owner, and it had been refurbished with a king-size oak bedroom suite, cobalt-blue drapes and a blue-and-cream striped duvet.

From there she moved on to the other guest room, where she found that the twin beds were draped with sheets, and the floorboards were bare, the bay window uncurtained. Three pristine cans of paint were stacked by the closet, along with paintbrushes, a roller and a paint tray.

Matt, it seemed, was planning to redecorate.

It *hurt*, to have an outsider brashly take possession of her home. And added to the hurt, was a spurt of anger. By rights, this house didn't even belong to Matt.

She marched into her own bedroom and irritably gathered up a pile of clothing that needed to be washed, items she'd accumulated during her cross-country car trip.

The laundry room was in the basement, and she found it just as tidy as the rest of the house. The white-tiled floor was spotless, the washer and dryer gleamed and a pile of folded but unironed clothing sat on the ironing board.

On a shelf above the ironing board was a box of Tide. Liz moved over to get it, but when she glanced absently at the pile of folded clothing, she came to an abrupt halt.

And with lips compressed she glared at the wispy lace bra so brazenly snuggled up to a pair of navy cotton boxer shorts.

It didn't take an Einstein to figure out what this meant. It couldn't have been more obvious, Liz reflected scornfully, if Matt had put a sign above his bed that read:

Molly Martin Has Slept Here!

Matt leaned against the veranda railing and looked down at Molly, who was lounging back in one of her Adirondack chairs. "You never mentioned," he said, "that you and Max Rossiter's daughter had been school friends."

"It just never came up." Molly put a hand over her eyes to block out the sun as she squinted up at him. "After Dad was transferred and our family moved to Vancouver, she and I did keep in touch a while but our letters eventually dribbled off. It wasn't till after my Dave was posted here four years ago that I really thought about her again. I did mean to get in touch once we were settled, but then I heard that after high school her dad had sent her off to some fancy college back east and she'd never come home again. Nobody seemed to know where she was…so…I let it slide."

Beth's father hadn't sent Beth off to college—at

least if he had, it hadn't been straight away; but he'd come up with that story because he hadn't wanted his family name besmirched. The truth was, he'd sent her somewhere else, and though he'd refused to tell Matt where, he'd taken a vicious delight in telling him why.

"Did you think," Max Rossiter had shouted at him on that black, never-to-be-forgotten autumn night, "that I would allow my daughter to let her pregnancy run its course so she could give birth to a child by the likes of *you*? You think I'd have let you ruin her *life*, her *future*? She's a Rossiter, boy, and you're *nothing*. You're *nobody!*"

Matt would never forget the hatred in the man's eyes. It had reminded him of the bloodshot frenzy of a raging bull.

Molly had been right, though; none of the townsfolk knew where "the rich Rossiter girl" had gone. And as far as he was aware, only four local people had ever known of her pregnancy—Beth, himself, his mother...and Beth's father.

"Matt?" Molly prodded his ankle with the toe of her sandal. "What is it? What are you thinking?"

He dragged his thoughts to the present. "I knew her, too, Molly. I knew Max Rossiter's daughter years ago...when she was seventeen."

"But...how? You would have been away at law school!"

"I came home to work in Judd Anstruther's law offices in the summer break and I met her a few weeks before she graduated from high school. In early June. And we hung around together, till I went back to UBC in the Fall."

"You and Beth Rossiter...you *dated?*"

"Yeah."

"But…nobody has ever mentioned it—you'd think that in all this time somebody would have mentioned it to me."

"Nobody knew. We had to keep it quiet, meet in secret. Because of her father. He didn't think any of us locals were good enough for his daughter. He had bigger—and better—plans for her."

For a minute or two, neither of them spoke. From down the street, Matt could hear Iain and Stuart shouting as they played with their friend Jamie.

Finally Molly said, "If you let her stay on at Laurel House, I'm afraid you're going to have your hands full."

"I'm not sure I…know what you mean…"

"I'm a nurse, Matt—or at least I was, and I know all the signs. I know that…look."

He stared at her, and felt a growing sense of dread that chilled him. "She…Liz…she isn't *ill,* is she?"

Molly closed her eyes and leaned her head back against the slats of the chair. "No, she isn't ill, Matt… She's pregnant."

Pregnant!

The word was still rolling around in Matt's head when he left Molly's an hour later.

But maybe Molly was mistaken. He latched onto the possibility…then reluctantly dismissed it when he recalled the confident tone she'd used when she'd added that she was very rarely wrong in such matters.

So Liz was—very likely—pregnant.

What should he do? Should he ask her outright if she was expecting a baby? Or should he give her an opening and wait for her to volunteer the information?

By the time he got back to Laurel House, he still

hadn't made up his mind what to do, so in the end he decided to play it by ear.

He parked the car and went inside. He was shutting the front door behind him when he heard her footsteps on the stairs. And by the time he'd walked into the foyer, she was almost at the bottom.

She stopped on the last step and looked at him warily.

"Hi," he said, assessing her with new eyes in light of what Molly had told him. "How's it going?"

She was all skin and bone and long arms and longer legs, but if her waist had thickened at all he had no way of telling because the pink silk blouson top she was wearing over her cream miniskirt gave nothing away.

He scrutinized her face, searching for whatever telltale signs Molly had seen. Was it the heaviness of her eyes? The tightly drawn skin over her nose? The tiny break-out of a rash on one smooth temple?

Dammit, he didn't *know* what the first signs of pregnancy were!

Liz put a hand on the newel post and frowned across at him.

"What's the matter?" Her voice rang with challenge. "Why on earth are you *staring* at me like that?"

CHAPTER FOUR

MATT saw, with a feeling of disappointment, that she was still in the hostile mood she'd been in last night.

Hoping to ease her out of it, he said lightly, "I was just thinking that you suit that color. What is it? Cherry blossom pink?"

"As I recall," she said dryly, "the store tag described it as Sunset Blush."

"Whatever, you look great in it. Elegant," he added with a grin, "as a pink flamingo!"

"Thank you. I think!" Although her cheeks had flushed two shades deeper than Sunset Blush, her eyes were cool.

"So," he said, "what have you been doing?"

"Just looking around." She smoothed a tidying hand down her hair; unnecessarily, since—to him at least—it looked perfect. "Getting the feel of things again."

"I used to do the same, whenever I came home from UBC in the summer holidays—I always had to wander around, looking, touching—though it didn't take long, our house being so small!" He saw her pink-glossed lips tighten and realized it had been a mistake to talk about summer vacation from UBC. Quickly he moved on. "Fancy some lemonade?"

She hesitated for a moment, and then with a shrug in her voice, said, "Sure."

In the kitchen, he took two cans of lemonade from

the fridge, poured hers into a glass and handed it to her.

He leaned against the counter, taking a draught from his can, while she perched on the edge of the table.

"Where did you get to this morning?" he asked.

"I went to church."

"Didn't see you there."

"I was late, took a seat at the back. I'd run out of gas, couldn't get the car started. I had to walk."

"And after?"

"I didn't hang around. I'm not quite ready to talk to people yet." She looked down at her glass, ran a slender fingertip over the rim. Her oval nails were painted the exact same shade of Sunset Blush as her lips. "Although I did have a word with an old friend on my way home. Molly White. Martin now. She said you were going to her place for lunch."

"She mentioned that you'd met up." He looked again at her hair, which was full of bits of sunshine from the rays streaming in through the window. It used to be a short curly mop; now it was parted in the center and fell to her breasts, straight as rain. He preferred it like this. Except that it made him ache to run his hands through it, to feel the silky strands slide through his fingers—

"Molly told me she'd lost her husband. How long ago was that?"

"Three years ago. He was a cop. Shot in the line of duty—got in the way of a bullet when he was trying to stop a robbery at the Esso station on Wayberry Road. He and Molly..." Matt shook his head. "They were so right for each other. She took it hard. As did the kids, of course. Stuart and Iain adored their dad.

And Dave thought the world of them, too. His family was his life."

"Does Molly have a job?"

"No. She trained as a nurse, though, in Vancouver. Worked there full-time till the kids came along, then part-time after that. She'd been planning to start full-time again, once both boys were in school...but before she could, Dave was killed. She was shattered, went totally to pieces. She hasn't worked at all since then. I often think it would be the best thing for her, to go back, but..." He shrugged.

He didn't tell Liz that he *wished* Molly would go back to work. It wasn't that he minded "being there" for her, he didn't. What concerned him was that instead of becoming less dependent on him as time went by, she was becoming more and more clingy, more and more needy. He'd expected that by now she'd be making moves to reclaim her independence. She hadn't. But he'd promised Dave to look after her for as long as she needed him. And so he would.

"Liz," he said, "I want to talk about *you*. Why did you come back here? Did things go...wrong...in New York?"

"Wrong? What do you mean?"

"You know...problems at work, or with...a man...?"

"That's my business, Matt. I'd prefer if you didn't try to pry into my affairs—"

"It's just that you're looking a bit...run-down."

"I was in a stressful job," she said. "I worked for the CEO of a major stockbroking firm. Busy, busy, busy, with long hours, constant deadlines. It took a lot out of me, I was getting burned out...but now that I'm home, I'll be fine. And since you're into making personal remarks,'' she added, raking a pointed glance over his face, ''it looks as if you finally met your match!''

She was referring, of course, to his broken nose; his scarred lip; his bashed-in cheekbone.

''Yeah.'' He managed to keep his tone nonchalant, but his hand clenched around the can and he heard a faint creak as the tin gave way under the pressure. ''I guess I did.''

''That must have hurt,'' she said. ''Your pride, too,'' she added facetiously.

''No,'' he said, ''not my pride.''

''So what are you saying? 'You should have seen the other guy'?''

''The other guy,'' he said, ''didn't have a mark on him.''

She raised her eyebrows, her expression mocking. ''Then you must *really* have met your match! Do you still fight?''

''No,'' he said. ''That was the very last time.''

''You lost the touch?''

''No, Liz. I didn't lose the touch. What I lost that night was the heart.''

Liz spent the rest of the day alone as Matt had arranged to go rock climbing with friends. Before heading off, he'd told her he wouldn't be back till late, so she cooked herself a light supper around six, and then watched TV for a while before tiredly going upstairs to bed.

But once in bed, she couldn't sleep for thinking about the conversation she and Matt had had that afternoon. She tossed and turned, unable to forget the look that had been in his eyes and the sorrowful tone

that had been in his voice when he'd spoken those
eight simple words.

What I lost that night was the heart.

The frankness and unexpectedness of his admission
had thrown her, and for a few long moments she'd
just stared at him. Then gathering herself together
she'd said flippantly,

"Then you fought over a woman."

"Yeah," he said. "A woman."

Jealousy wasn't an admirable emotion, nor was it a
comfortable one. Liz had struggled against its on-
slaught. "She was pretty?"

"No, she was beautiful. To me, she was the most
beautiful woman in the world."

"And you were in love with her."

"Yeah."

"How much?" Liz didn't know what had driven
her to ask the question; all she knew was, she had to
ask it. Why? To *torture* herself?

He was smiling at her in a way that gave her goose
bumps, his mouth twisted but his eyes devoid of humor.

"How much?" he asked. "More than I've ever
loved anyone else. More than I ever *will* love anyone
else. She didn't just steal my heart. She *was* my
heart."

Liz felt her eyes smart. And she turned away to hide
her tears. But he must have spotted them because as
she set her can on the table, he said, quietly, "Why
are you crying?"

She blinked the tears away before she faced him
again.

"I just feel sorry for you. To have lost a person you

loved that much...it must have been hard. Was it a long time ago?''

''Years ago.''

''So...you're over her now?''

''No, I'm not over her. I doubt I ever will be. She was the only one for me.''

Liz heard a whimper. But even as the sound jolted her, she realized she wasn't in the kitchen, talking to Matt, but in her bed, alone.

And at the same time, she realized she had to get up.

One of the joys of pregnancy, she reflected as she pushed aside the covers, was this frequent need to go to the bathroom—and it was a need that disturbed most of her nights.

Switching on the bedside lamp she glanced at the clock radio on the night table. Two o'clock! And she hadn't yet slept a wink.

She padded across the room, and after opening the door very quietly, she crept along the corridor to the bathroom.

But when she tried to turn the knob, she found it was locked. She would have to go downstairs to the powder room. She was about to turn away when the door opened suddenly.

''Sorry,'' Matt said. ''You wanted in here?''

In the bright light from the corridor she could see that his hair was wet. She could also see he was wearing nothing but a navy towel wrapped precariously around his hips. His chest was damp, and a single drop of water ran down one bare arm.

''Have you been *showering?*'' she asked, and wished she'd taken a moment to put on her robe. Her

pink silk nightie was skimpy as a handkerchief and
covered about as much.

"Yeah," he said. "A cold one."

"A *cold* one?"

"It's hot tonight. Or hadn't you noticed? I couldn't
sleep so I took a shower to cool off. But seeing you
in that sexy next-to-nothing slip," he went on straight-
faced, "I may have to take another one!"

"Don't be a smart aleck!" she shot back. "Now if
you'll let me past I'll—"

He caught her arm as she tried to slide by him. His
fingers were cool on her heated skin

"How come *you're* up so late?" he asked. "Are
you okay? I thought I heard you moving around a
couple of times before."

She couldn't be sure how much Matt knew about
the minor inconveniences of pregnancy, but she wasn't
about to give him any clues as to her condition.

"I'm a night wanderer," she said vaguely, shrugging off his hand. "It's a habit I picked up in New
York."

"Ah, New York." He leaned back against the doorjamb. "I've never been to the Big Apple. Since neither
of us can sleep, why don't we take a stroll in the
moonlight and you can tell me all about life in the
city. We could bring a bottle of wine—"

"I don't think that's a good idea."

"Why? You don't like wine?"

She enjoyed an occasional glass of
Chardonnay…but she couldn't tell him that in light of
her pregnancy, she didn't drink wine. Maybe he knew
that expectant moms should abstain from alcohol,
maybe he didn't. But she didn't want him putting two
and two together.

"Oh, sure, I enjoy wine. But not at this time of night. Actually—" she faked a wide yawn "—I'm feeling a bit sleepy now. I think if I get back to bed, I'll drop off soon. Do you mind…?"

He pushed himself from the doorjamb and waved her forward into the bathroom. "No," he said, "you go ahead. But remember," he added, "anytime you fancy a walk in the moonlight and want company…my offer's open."

And that was one offer, she decided as she locked the bathroom door behind her, that she'd be very wise to forget!

Matt made a practice of going in to the office early.

And especially on summer mornings, when he enjoyed the quietness of the street and the dewy scents that the breezes drifted to him from the hanging baskets that were part of Tradition's Beautification Project—a project his mother had spearheaded two years before.

But on this Monday morning, he barely noticed his surroundings, he was too engrossed in thoughts of Liz.

He hadn't been lying when he'd told her he ought to have a second cold shower after seeing her in that skimpy pink nightie. He *had* been lying, though, when he told her he'd taken the first shower to cool off from the hot summer night. He'd really taken it because he couldn't sleep for thinking about her—torturing himself with memories of how it had been between them, memories of the passion they'd shared, memories of her smooth, lithe body entwined with his.

But if she was pregnant, her body wouldn't be lithe for too much longer. She would put on weight, she would grow heavy and awkward. And she would need help.

If only, he mused as he walked into his office, she were as clingy as Molly had become. And if only Molly were as independent as Liz. His life would be so much easier.

"Good morning, Mr. Garvock."

"Good morning, Frannie." He threw his receptionist an appreciative smile as he came alongside her desk. Frannie, too, liked to get a head start on the day. But unlike him, she made a point of always leaving work at four-thirty sharp. And he had no quarrel with that. She had a husband and five children and her home schedule was hectic.

He knew all about her family life because she lived next door to Molly, and the two were close friends.

"Did you have a good weekend?" he asked, looking down at the message slips she handed him.

"We took the kids to the water-slide park, had a ball. And how about you?" Her eyes had an expectant glitter. "I talked with Molly when she got home from church yesterday. She was rushing into the house to check the roast, but she was really excited, said you were coming over for a special lunch?"

She finished on a questioning note, and the eagerness in her eyes confused him. "Yeah," he said. "She made a lovely meal, best roast beef I've had in a while."

"And...?"

"And...what?"

"Well?" Frannie seemed to be bursting with excitement, but over what, Matt hadn't a clue. Before he could ask, her phone rang.

She picked it up and was immediately all business.

After a brief conversation with the person on the other end of the line, she pressed the Hold button and said,

"It's Des Hunter, Mr. Garvock. He wants to talk to you about his rezoning application for the Brown property."

"Thanks, Fran."

Matt strode into his office, and sitting down on the swivel chair behind his desk, he picked up his phone.

Seconds later, he was deeply involved in a discussion with his client, and had dismissed his receptionist's puzzling attitude and comments from his mind.

Liz woke to the sound of fiendish screaming.

She lay wide-eyed, heartbeats racing. Was someone committing murder? But even as she asked herself the question, she realized that what she was hearing wasn't someone yelling out in mortal agony; it was the skirl of bagpipes wailing out some ancient Scottish lament.

She sat up and shoved back her hair. Glancing at the clock, she grimaced. Okay, so she had slept late. But still...Matt Garvock was the most inconsiderate man she'd ever met. He *knew* she'd had a restless night yet he was inflicting this nerve-rasping torture on her.

She got off the bed and snatching up her robe, put it on as she marched out of the room. If playing that wild heathen music was a ploy to get rid of her, he would have to try another tack.

The sound was coming from the empty guest room.

She stamped across the lobby and through the doorway...

And stopped short.

A skinny, ponytailed painter wearing a back-to-front baseball cap and paint-spattered white dungarees was standing atop a ladder with his back to her. On the window seat lay the offending ghetto blaster, its stereo beat so loud it was like having rusty nails hammered in her ears.

She crossed the room and snapped the Off switch down. Then, fisting her hands on her hips, she turned to confront the painter...who had swiveled around, paintbrush poised in one hand, and was staring down at her with startled eyes.

Before Liz could speak, he said, in a voice that was high with astonishment, "Who are you?" He gaped at Liz, his eyes widening as he scanned her sleep-mussed hair, her short robe, her long bare legs and her bare feet.

Liz felt her hackles rise at the man's blatant show of interest. She drew in a deep breath preparing to let fly at him...but the air was laden with the smell of paint and noxious fumes and all of a sudden she felt dizzy. Fighting against a queasy feeling, she pressed a hand to her stomach.

"Please stop what you're doing," she ordered. "There's been a misunderstanding. Mr. Garvock had no right to order any work done here so I'd like you to pack up and—"

The room was spinning. She was going to be sick.

She swung away toward the door and by the time she reached the bathroom, she was running.

She made it to the toilet just in time. And sinking to the floor, she grabbed the edge of the seat and started heaving. But her stomach was empty and nothing came up. She felt sweat bead her brow, felt her skin turn clammy—

And then she felt firm hands grasp her shoulders. Felt them steady her as she retched and twisted.

"Hang on," the painter said. "You'll be okay."

Okay? She'd never be okay again. Last time around her morning sickness had passed after the first trimester, but so far this time it showed no signs of letting up. She felt as if she were dying! And she should have been *outraged* that this stranger had followed her into the privacy of the bathroom...but, she admitted weakly, it did help to have his hands steadying her.

After several long minutes, the attack of nausea passed. She pushed herself up, and the man stood back.

She stumbled to the sink, where she splashed icy water over her face. Then she reached blindly to the rail for a towel...but found one thrust into her hands.

She dabbed her face dry, and then leaning shakily back against the sink, she opened her eyes.

The painter was looking at her, his smile sympathetic.

"Feeling better now?" He took the towel from her, and slung it over the rack. But Liz's startled gaze had stayed glommed to the painter's face, taking in, for the first time, the slate-gray shadow that enhanced the green eyes, and the dark mascara coating the long, feathery lashes.

The painter, she realized belatedly, was a woman!

"Yes," she said stiffly. "I'm fine. And thank you for your help but I'd appreciate if you'd pack up your gear and leave."

The woman hooked her thumbs into her dungaree straps. "I can't. I have to see this job through. Unless I hear otherwise—" her tone was amused "—from the gaffer."

She was as irritating as a hangnail. Liz scowled at her. Should she try to evict her, bodily, from the house? The painter wasn't much *bigger* than she was...but she looked wiry and tough. Besides, it wouldn't be wise to get into a brawl, not when she had the baby to consider.

The woman wasn't about to hang around waiting for a response. Throwing Liz a friendly smile, she walked away and returned to the guest room.

The skirl of bagpipes wailed through the house once more, and Liz pressed her hands to her ears as she hurried back to her room to look for the clothes she'd wear for her confrontation with "the gaffer"!

"How may I help you?" The receptionist ran an assessing gaze over Liz's smart navy suit as she approached the desk.

Liz looked around. To the right she saw a door with a brass plate bearing Matt's name.

"I'd like to see Mr. Garvock, please."

"You don't have an appointment—"

"He'll see me. Just tell him Ms. Rossiter is here."

"I'm afraid I can't do—"

Liz started determinedly toward his door.

"Mr. Garvock," the voice cooed after her, "has gone out for lunch."

With a "Tsk!" of annoyance, Liz turned.

"Look," she said. "This can't wait. I need to see him now. Where can I find him? Which restaurant?"

The receptionist hesitated.

"It really is important," Liz said.

Sighing, the woman sat back. "He sent out for coffee and a sandwich and he said he was going to eat lunch over in Elmoor Park, since it was such a nice day.''

"Thank you," Liz said. "I appreciate your help."

Three minutes later she was walking through the open gates of the riverside park. She spotted Matt right away. He was sitting sprawled out on a bench, his arms relaxed along the back of the bench, his long legs thrust out and crossed at the ankle, his face up to the sun, his eyes closed against its brilliant noon-hour glare.

Her heartbeats staggered...but she herself did not. She marched toward him on the narrow path, her pumps clicking briskly on the sunbaked cement.

Matt paid no heed to the approaching sound. Only when she came to a halt in front of the bench, within kicking distance of his big Nikes, did he cock one eye lazily open.

His eyelids flickered, but it was the only sign she saw of his surprise.

"Why didn't you tell me," she snapped, "that you were having a workperson in the house this morning?"

He grinned. "A work*person*. Well, I guess that coming from the big city, you have to make sure you're politically correct. Here in this old town we—"

"I am not—" she bulldozed over top of him "—here to talk about what is or is not politically correct. I'm here to talk about your painter and her ghetto blaster. I did *not* appreciate being wakened up to the sound of skirling bagpipes—"

"Ah, yes, it would be the bagpipes." Laughter bubbled in his voice. "You see, our work*person* has taken up genealogy and she discovered a few weeks ago, to her great delight, that her great-great-grandmother on her mother's side was a Campbell. From Argyll, no less. And ever since, she's been steeping herself in—"

"She can steep herself in single malt whiskey for all I care!" Liz tried to keep her cool, but he was really being impossible. "And she can drape herself in tartan and eat haggis till it's coming out of her ears…only, not in my house! I told her to leave but she's dug her heels in. She says she won't quit the job till she gets the order from the 'gaffer' himself. And I guess—" she stuck her hands on her hips "—the 'gaffer' would be you!"

He was laughing at her. Oh, not out loud, but she could see the merriness in his eyes.

He stood, and she took a step back. Even in her heels, she felt tiny beside him. And vulnerable.

"We have to talk," he said. And now his face had become serious. "But it's too hot out here. Let's go back to my office. It's air-conditioned."

She tried not to notice how snugly his white T-shirt stretched over his hard-muscled chest; and she tried even harder not to notice how shamefully her body was responding to his sexy scent, pheromones and sandalwood and fresh male sweat, a potent mix guaranteed to fell a woman at twenty paces.

And she was *much* closer than that. Feeling dizzy, she put a hand to her temple, and began to sway.

Matt grabbed her arm. "Let's get you inside, out of this heat—and I'll fix you up with a nice cool drink."

Liz didn't protest. She knew if he took his supporting hand away, she might well drop to the ground like a pat of melted butter!

Matt leaned his hip on the edge of his desk and watched narrowly as Liz sat back in an armchair and sipped iced tea.

Seeing her in the park had surprised him—especially because he'd been thinking about her, and with
such intensity he'd actually wondered, when she materialized in front of him, if he had conjured her up
out of his own mind.

But no, it had been Liz in the flesh. And she'd
looked so sexy in that prim navy suit with her flaxen
hair tightly coiled up, she'd taken his breath away. She
didn't know it, of course. He guessed her intention had
been to present a buttoned-up image; what she *didn't*
realize was that what she presented was a temptation.
An irresistible temptation. What he ached to do was
uncoil that silky topknot, unravel that glossy hair, open
each button of that suit jacket—

"You said we had to talk. What did you want to
say?"

He wanted to say that he'd had a phone call half an
hour ago from the painter work*person*…and the call
had seemed to confirm what Molly had told him yesterday. And he wanted to say that while he'd been
sitting in the park, he'd come up with a plan.

But before he got to that, he first had to find out if
Liz really was pregnant. He was pretty sure she was,
and he was going to call her on it. Right now.

Pushing himself from the desk he stood straight.

"Liz." He hoped to hell he was right, or he was
going to appear like the biggest fool on the face of the
earth. "I know you want to fight me for your family
home, and I can't stop you from doing that. It's your
decision—"

"Well, thank you!" Her tone was sarcastic.

"—but I suggest you postpone taking any action—"

"No way." Her eyes had taken on a steely determination. "I'm going to take action *now*."

"—for at least a few months until you're more able to cope. Court fights can be extremely stressful and you've already admitted you're burned out. I'd go further, I'd say you're on your way to cracking up. Take it easy, take a break—"

Her eyes flashed sparks and she opened her mouth to shout him down. He didn't give her a chance.

"—if not for you own sake," he finished steadily, "then do it for the sake of your unborn child."

CHAPTER FIVE

Liz stared disbelievingly at Matt.

How on earth had he discovered she was pregnant?

She leaned over and set her glass on the low coffee table in front of her, stealing a moment to steady herself.

When she looked up again, she had schooled her features into an emotionless mask.

"My pregnancy," she said, "has nothing to do with you." Old wounds, still painful, made her cruel. *"This time."*

She saw his Adam's apple jerk convulsively.

"But this time," he said, "you want to *keep* the baby."

Her fingers trembled. She twined them together in her lap. "Of *course* I want to keep my baby. I don't know what you mean...what do you mean? What are you trying to say?"

He sighed. "I'm sorry. That was unfair." He crossed to the window, and stood looking out, though he saw nothing of the wide street, nor the hanging baskets, which usually gave him such pleasure. His eyes were blurred as his mind got tangled up in anguished memories. "I know I let you down. I know that if I'd been the man I should have been, we'd have stood up together to your father when he forbade you to have my child, and you'd never have let him send you away or let him force you to have an—"

"What are you talking about?"

61

He swiveled around abruptly as he heard the grating edge to Liz's voice.

She had lurched to her feet and her eyes were stark with horror. "What are you saying, Matt? You think I didn't want our baby, you think I—"

He closed the space between them and grabbed her shoulders. "Liz, you don't have to defend what you did. You don't have to explain why you—"

"Matt, my father didn't *send* me away. He wasn't going to let me go through with my pregnancy so I *ran* away. I would never have let anyone take our baby from me, I ran away because I so desperately wanted to keep it...but in the end," she said chokingly, "I *lost* it anyway." She wrenched herself free and staggered back, coming up against the wall and staring at him as if she didn't even recognize him. "Are you telling me that all these years you thought I—"

"It was what your father told me." Stunned, Matt stared back at her. Was it really true? Had Max Rossiter lied to him? But worse than that...if those had indeed been lies, he, Matt, had believed them.

"Liz." He didn't know what to do. What to say. He could hardly bear to look at her. Her eyes were swimming with tears—tears of incredulity, tears of hurt, tears of betrayal that tore at his heart. "Oh, sweetheart, I—"

"I am not your *sweetheart.*" Furiously she brushed away her tears with the back of her hands. "I'm nobody's sweetheart." She realized she was shouting. "Least of all, *yours!*"

She spun away toward the door, but before she got there, she felt light-headed, and saw gold stars suddenly dance and swim in the air in front of her. Dizzily she fumbled for the doorknob but before she could find it, a black curtain descended slowly over her eyes.

It was the last thing she was aware of before she crumpled, in a heap, to the floor.

Like a caged cougar, Matt prowled the waiting room at the Medical Center, occasionally pausing to glower at Dr. Black's firmly closed door. Liz had been in there for almost half an hour. What the devil was going on? And how much longer did the doctor need, to find out what was wrong with her?

Fortunately the clinic was situated directly across the street from his own office and he'd lost no time in carrying Liz across the way when she'd passed out. Featherlight in his arms, and limper than wet paper, she'd begun to come to as they entered the clinic, and by the time they'd reached the reception desk, she was demanding to be put down.

He'd given in, but he'd been mightily relieved when Alex Black had whisked Liz straight into his office.

Where she'd been ever since.

Matt turned now to the receptionist, Sandy Webster, a pleasant redhead he'd known since high school.

"What the *devil's* going on in there?" he asked.

"Dr. Black's very thorough." Sandy tried to calm him with soothing words. "Ms. Rossiter's in very good hands, Matt. She should be coming out any minute now."

And at that, the office door opened.

Liz appeared, accompanied by the doctor.

"Thank you, Dr. Black," she said. "I'll see you again in two weeks, then."

"Make an appointment with Sandy before you leave." The doctor adjusted his rimless glasses. "Now remember…you *must* have lots of rest—a nap every afternoon, early to bed at night. And no housework, no gardening, no slaving over a hot stove! No exertion of *any* kind. Basically you're healthy enough but you've let yourself get run-down, and we have to build you up again.''

Liz was going to be fine. As Matt assimilated the welcome news, he felt his heart lighten.

He watched Liz move over to the desk and he noticed that her cheeks had more color, her eyes had a livelier spark.

She must be happy that everything was okay.

And the baby's father…would he be happy, too, when she told him? *Would* she tell him…or had she cut the guy completely out of her life, in the same way as she'd done with him? He wanted to know…but he didn't have the right to ask.

He had no rights where Liz Rossiter was concerned. Any rights he once had he had forfeited thirteen years before.

''Matt.''

He reined in his straying thoughts as the doctor addressed him. Dragging his gaze from Liz, who was taking an appointment card from Sandy, he said, ''Yeah, Alex?''

''Liz tells me she's staying at Laurel House. I'll be depending on you to look after her. See that she does what she's told—''

''Oh, you can count on it! I'll drive her home and make sure she—''

Liz materialized at his side and put a light hand on his forearm.

''Let's discuss this outside.'' Her smile was honey-sweet…on the surface. ''Shall we?''

"Sure." He said easily. "Let's do that."

She thanked the doctor again and then preceded Matt out to the street.

Once on the sidewalk, he said, "Where's your car?"

"I walked. You may recall I ran out of gas and—"

"Oh, yeah. I was going to bring home a container of gas tonight and—"

"Thank you," she said, "for offering to drive me home. I'll take you up on that, because I don't want to risk passing out on the road, which I might well do if I were to walk. But we'll stop at a gas station on the way, and I'll buy a can of gas for my car—"

"No."

"No?"

"No. Dr. Black has put you in my care, and if you need to go anywhere, I'll drive you. At least, for the next couple of weeks, till you go back for your checkup."

She opened her mouth to protest, but when he said, quietly, "For the baby's sake, Liz. It would be best."

He could see the frustration in her expression, and knew how hemmed in she felt by the limitations her condition had placed on her. But in the end, she said, reluctantly, "You're probably right. Just for the next couple of weeks, though, and then I want to get around on my own."

"Agreed. *If* the doc gives you the go-ahead."

While they'd been talking he'd led her to his car. Now he opened the door and he helped her inside.

As they made their way up the street, she said, "We have to talk. About the house."

"We will." He put his signal out and turned left at the end of the block. "I have to go back to the office till around four, but I'll be home as soon as I can get away. In the meantime, you'll follow doctor's orders and go for an afternoon nap. Take it easy. Avoid stress.''

His eyes were on the road but he could feel her stiffen.

"I don't need you to give me advice, Matt."

He flicked a frowning glance her way. She was staring ahead, and her profile was forbidding.

"You and I," he said, "and any differences we have or may have had...they're not important now. What's important is your baby. As I've said before, I'm not your enemy. I want only what's best for you. I'm not about to browbeat you, or make you try to do things you'd rather not. And I'll try not to give you advice you don't want. But I do have a plan in mind, one I hope you'll find acceptable. I'll tell you what that plan is. Tonight."

"There's one thing," she said, "that I want settled right now."

"Sure," he said. "What is it?"

"That painter. The one who fancies herself as a kilted warrior marching up and down the glens of Argyll..."

"Yeah? What about her?"

They had reached the driveway leading up to Laurel House. As Matt slowed the car and then coasted to a halt by the front steps of the house, Liz turned to him.

"She has to go." Her eyes flashed. "Will you please find her and fire her?"

Out of the corner of his eye, he saw an overalled figure come out the front door.

He hid a smile.

"There she is," he said, gesturing toward the

woman who had paused at the top of the steps. He pushed open his door and strode around the Taurus to open Liz's. He offered her a hand and though she allowed him to help her out, as soon as she was upright she slipped her fingers free.

He cupped her elbow and led her to the foot of the shallow steps, where he came to a stop.

His smile was mischievous as his gaze flicked from one woman to the other. "I gather you two haven't been formally introduced."

"So do it!" Liz hissed. "Tell her she's toast!"

"Naomi." His tone held a ripple of amusement. "I'd like you to meet Max Rossiter's daughter, Lizbeth Rossiter. Liz—" he turned to the woman standing rigidly by his side because not for anything in the world would he have missed the expression on her face when he completed the introduction "—I'd like you to meet my mother, Naomi Garvock."

Liz lay back in her bed, savoring the cool sheets, the soft white pillows, the shadowy darkness of the room.

She felt oddly detached from the world; and cocooned.

Outside, she could hear the liquid *slip-lip tsit-tsit* of barn swallows as they swooped and dove under the eaves; and she could hear voices outside, followed by the slam of a car door, then the sound of an engine starting up.

Matt. Going back to the office.

The house was quiet.

She wanted to sleep, but her mind was too busy processing everything that had happened since she first woke up that morning.

The bagpipe-loving painter was Matt's mother.

What a surprise that had been! And Liz was well aware of how much fun Matt had got out of that situation; but not in any nasty way, just taking a delight at having been able to stick a pin in her pomposity.

As for Naomi Garvock...she couldn't have been warmer, friendlier. She hadn't held a grudge...in fact, she'd gone as far as to chastise her son for what she called his juvenile sense of humor—

Liz jumped as someone tapped on her bedroom door.

Swallowing, she pushed herself up on one elbow.

"Who...is it?" she asked. And held her breath.

The door opened tentatively. "It's just me..."

It was Matt's mother. And she was carrying a small tray, with a steaming teapot, two stoneware mugs, a plate of cookies.

"I thought," Naomi Garvock said with a smile as she padded across the room in her white socks, "that you might enjoy a cuppa. You've had quite a day. Besides, I never did apologize for waking you up so rudely this morning!"

She set the tray on the night table and then saying, "Sit up, dear," she leaned behind Liz, tugged up her pillows and tilted them against the headboard. "There, now, lean back, make yourself comfy, and I'll pour our tea. I hope," she added, "that you like peppermint flavor?"

Liz felt as if she were being steamrollered but she didn't have the strength to get out from under. "Thanks," she said, sinking weakly back against the pillows. "I thought you had left with Matt—I didn't see another car when we drove up earlier."

"I came by bike." She handed Liz one of the mugs.

"I don't have a car." She offered the cookie plate but Liz shook her head.

"No, thanks, Mrs. Garvock. I'm not really hungry."

"Call me Naomi. Everybody does." She put down the cookie plate and as she picked up her own mug, she said casually, "May I call you Liz?"

"Of course." Liz took in a deep breath. "I want to apologize," she said, "for my display of bad manners this morning. You must have thought I was a spoiled brat!"

"What I thought—" Naomi's green eyes twinkled "—was that my son had spent the night with a rather beautiful young woman, so I have to apologize, too— for thinking sinful thoughts! I was away for the weekend, you see, and hadn't talked to Matt since Friday. I had no idea you had turned up and were staying here. And even if I had, I probably wouldn't have recognized you. It's been a long time."

"Yes, it has."

"Liz...I want you to know that Matt told me, after you went upstairs to bed, about...what happened to you, after you left town thirteen years ago. I knew, you see, that you were pregnant—although my son didn't confide in me until a while later. I just want you to know how dreadfully sorry I am that you lost the baby. What a heartbreaking time that must have been for you."

At the compassion in Naomi's voice, Liz felt the smart of tears. "It's over now," she said quietly. "And the doctors told me that what happened was for the best. But this time around, the baby's heartbeat is very strong and according to Dr. Black I have nothing to worry about. I just have to take it easy and try to build myself up a bit."

"How did you get along with Dr. Black?"

"I liked him right away. He seems very competent."

"He is."

For a few minutes they sipped their tea in companionable silence, then Naomi said,

"Do you find it…difficult…to be here, in this house, now that…Matt owns it?"

Since Matt's mother was being very open and honest with her, Liz decided to be equally frank. "My father had no right to sell this place. And I do have something in writing that will prove it. So…to answer your question, I do find the present situation difficult…but I do intend to fight Matt for Laurel House."

Naomi looked startled, and Liz realized that Matt couldn't have told his mother anything of their conflict over the property. But all Naomi said was, "Well, I'm sure you and Matt will sort it out between you, one way or the other. You're both mature adults. Now," she indicated the empty mug in Liz's hand, "if you'll let me have that, I'll leave and let you have some sleep."

She set Liz's mug with her own on the tray, and lifting the tray, walked over to the door where she paused and turned.

"By the way, Matt has told me to leave the painting, for now. But I do come around every few days to tidy the place for Matt and do the laundry and stock up his fridge, so if there's anything you need, anything at all, just make a list and I'll be happy to attend to it for you."

"Mrs. Garvock, you don't have to—"

"Naomi. And no, I don't have to…but I want to.

Now you lie back, try to sleep. And Matt'll be home before you know it.''

Matt closed the front door, set his briefcase on the bench across from the hall closet and made his way to the foot of the stairs. Cocking his head to one side, he listened, but all he heard was silence.

Was Liz asleep?

With carefully quiet steps, he climbed the stairs, and crossed the landing. Her bedroom door was open. Sunlight poured in through the open blinds and he saw that the room was empty.

As he turned back, the bathroom door opened and she appeared. He saw her give a start when she saw him.

"Sorry," he said quickly. "I didn't mean to frighten you. I'd have made more noise to alert you as I came upstairs, but I was afraid you might have been asleep."

She was wearing a white shirt and taupe pedal pushers, and her hair skimmed over her shoulders in two symmetrical white-gold swathes. She could have passed for twenty...but for the weary look in her eyes, which today were more pearl-gray than khaki, reflecting the light from her shirt.

"I was," she said as she walked toward him. "I must have slept for a couple of hours."

"How are you feeling?"

"Not ready to run a marathon but okay."

"Ready to come downstairs?"

"Mmm."

He followed her as she descended the staircase. She trailed her left hand on the banister for support and he noticed that she wore no wedding band on her ring finger.

"Have you ever been married?" The question popped out before he took time to think.

She stiffened slightly but kept moving. And she didn't answer till they'd both reached the foot of the stairs. Then she turned and looked up at him.

"No," she said. "But I've been in love twice…with men who—I believed—cared for me, too. But although they both wanted to have sex with me, and both pledged their undying love…" She shrugged. "When push came to shove, they both left me hanging in the wind."

Matt flinched inside from the hard look in her eyes. He'd been *desperately* in love with her, and had just as desperately wanted to marry her…once he had graduated, had a job and was able to support her. But he'd just been a third-year student when she'd told him she was pregnant, and as a result he'd been devastated. Frantic. Distraught. Panic-stricken. And he'd said all the wrong things.

She'd taken off, weeping.

And by the time he'd got over his initial panic and come to his senses, it was too late. She'd disappeared.

Now she was back, and she was pregnant…again. And one thing his question had elicited was that she had loved the father of this child, too. But he, too, had let her down.

"So this baby's father isn't going to be in the picture?" he said.

"That's right. I'm on my own."

And it won't be the first time. She didn't say the words, she didn't need to; her cynical expression said it all.

"I want to talk about that," he said.

"I can't imagine what you could possibly say about my situation that would be of any interest to me!"

"Let's not argue about it right now. You shouldn't be standing around." He set his hand in the small of her back and steered her firmly across the foyer and into the sitting room. "I want you to rest on the patio, in the shade, while I make our dinner."

She came to a sudden halt. "I'm perfectly able to make my own din—"

He pressed a fingertip against her lips. "No slaving over a hot stove for you. Doctor's orders." Her full pink lips were soft and warm; he had to fight a sudden impulse to run his fingertip over the upper curve—

"You can *cook?*"

She'd reared her head back but just before she did her lips pouted against his finger for one brief moment.

It had felt like a kiss.

The sensation aroused him and when he replied to her question, his voice was rough.

"Well, I don't slave over a kitchen stove...but then I don't have to—the women in my life are determined to outdo each other in the catering department. But I can broil a damned good steak, and that's what you're going to have tonight. So—" he took her hand and tugged her across to the screen doors leading to the patio "—while I slave over a hot *barbecue,* you'll recline on a cushioned lounger and drink iced tea...and watch me."

"Do I have a choice?"

He slid open the screen door. "The only choice you'll have is whether you want your steak rare or medium or—as the best chefs refer to well-done steaks—ruined!"

*   *   *

Liz chose to have her steak medium, Matt had his rare. He served them with baked potatoes and sour cream, and a simple salad of butter lettuce and hothouse tomatoes, and Liz enjoyed every morsel.

As she sat back afterward, enjoying the long rays of the evening sun and sipping the last of her iced tea, she watched Matt clear away their dishes.

He'd changed earlier into khaki shorts and a navy tank top. His body was tanned and he looked fit. He had more hair on his chest than he'd had in his student days.

Not wanting to let her thoughts drift to the intimacy of their shared past, she dragged her gaze up. His brow was furrowed in concentration as he gathered up plates and barbecue tools; and she was able to study him without detection.

She'd already got used to his "new" face. And she'd decided it suited him. He'd been attractive before, of course, but in a more conventionally handsome way. Now…the broken nose gave his face character; the scarred lip gave it interest; and the flattened cheekbone gave it vulnerability. She found herself wanting to run her fingertips gently over the battered contours, "relearning" his features, the way a blind person might.

Who had his adversary been? she wondered again. Would she ever find out? But even as she asked herself the questions, she acknowledged that she didn't really care who he'd fought with; what she really wanted to know was the identity of the female they'd been battling over.

Jealousy made her heart ache—irrational jealousy, for although Matt had said the woman had been the only one for him, she herself had no intention of getting emotionally involved with Matt. He had let her down when she'd needed him most; if she ever gave in to her feelings for him, how could she ever be sure he wouldn't let her down again?

A clatter startled her. Matt had been trying to carry too much at once, and had dropped the barbecue tools, along with a small blue plastic bowl that was bouncing its merry way across the patio toward her.

She scooped it up, and held it out to him.

"The lazy man's burden," she said archly.

"What?" He scowled at her, but his mouth twitched at the corners.

"Trying to carry everything at once, to save time. But in the end, it's usually quicker to make two trips."

He took the bowl, perched it atop his load, and then crouching down, kept his eyes on her as he lifted the barbecue tools and added them to his pile.

"Just watch me," he said. And stepping gingerly over the patio, he nudged the screen door open with his knee.

"There," he said, and walked triumphantly into the sitting room.

Liz held her breath and listened. And then chuckled as, ten heartbeats later, she heard an almighty crash, followed almost immediately by a loud and heartfelt "Damn!"

Dr. Black had told her not to run around like a wild thing, but he had also said that gentle walks would do her good.

Liz eased herself up from her chaise, and wandered around the garden, pausing here as she remembered climbing this particular tree as a child…and there as she recalled scraping her knee badly on that particular rock…and finally stopping at the high stone wall at the foot of the garden, the wall she used to climb as an agile seventeen-year-old when she'd snuck out, after her father was asleep, to meet Matt on those wonderful moonlit summer nights.

Matt saw her there, with her hand set lightly atop the garden wall, when he came out of the house.

He stood for a moment on the patio, looking at her.

He could guess where her thoughts were. And his own thoughts, too, leaped back in time. How many nights had he waited, at the other side of that wall, for her curly blond head to appear in the moonlight? How many times had he caught her slender figure as she jumped down into his arms? How many times had they made love together, on the—

He saw that Liz had noticed him and had started walking up the path.

Fighting to wrestle his memories back where they belonged, he strolled down to join her. They met alongside the gazebo, its tangle of red rambling roses twining in profusion around the white-painted trellis-work.

"The garden's in good shape." Liz touched one of the scarlet blossoms. "Did you hire a gardener?"

"I cut the grass, do the pruning and heavy work, and my mother takes care of the weeding and such like."

"Once I get my house back," Liz said, "I'll be looking after the garden myself." Her tone was as determined as her stubbornly tilted chin. "Just as my mother did. And her mother before her and—"

"Liz—"

"—her mother before *her!* The baby will keep me

busy, but I'm sure I'll have lots of free time. Yes,'' she finished, her voice becoming shrill, "I'm looking forward to taking charge of my own garden *and my own house!*"

"Liz." He grasped her shoulders tightly, giving her no chance to shake herself free. "Listen to me. Can't you see how you're getting yourself all riled up? It's not good for you—or for your baby. I do understand how you feel. But I bought Laurel House legally, paid for it fair and square—"

"I have letters that prove my father had no right to sell! Letters my mother wrote to her best friend, Melissa, telling her she'd made my father promise to add my name to the house deeds when I was twenty-one...and I was actually there in the room with my parents when my mother told him he had to do it and I was there when he promised he would and—"

"Just listen to my plan. What I suggest is that you and I *both* live here—"

"No way!"

"—until after your baby is safely born. Then—if you still want to fight me—go ahead, I'll give you a run for your money...but at least I'll know I won't be endangering your health, or that of your unborn child. Will you," he said urgently, "at least give my plan your consideration?"

CHAPTER SIX

Liz shook her head.

"No, I'm going to move on this right away and—"

"Liz, please—"

"Don't hassle me, Matt." She stepped back from him as he reached out a hand in appeal. "I'm not going to change my mind."

"Will you at least sleep on it? I promise I won't pressure you any more this evening…in fact, I'm going out shortly."

"My answer would be the same in the morning."

"Then I'll accept it, in the morning."

She hesitated, and then finding herself unable to withstand his pleading expression, said, "Okay. But—"

"Just *think* about it, that's all I ask—"

"Matt, you just said you wouldn't pressure me!"

"Sorry. Okay, not another word on the subject."

They started walking up to the house together.

"Where are you off to tonight?" she asked.

"I'm taking Molly to a 'do' at the rec center—a fund-raiser for the baseball team."

"What kind of a 'do'?" She kept her tone light.

"A silent auction, followed by a dance."

Liz *liked* Molly and knew she should have been pleased that her widowed friend had found someone new to love. But instead, she felt her heart twist at the thought of Matt and Molly dancing close.

"In fact," Matt said, "I'd better get showered and changed. I have to be at Molly's in twenty minutes."

"Is the dance formal?"

"Uh-uh. It's a barn dance, anything goes."

They'd reached the patio and he turned to her.

"Are you coming in now?"

"No, I'll stay out till it cools off."

"Then what will you do?"

"Matt, please don't concern yourself about me. I'm perfectly able to look after myself."

"I just want you to take it easy. Remember what the doc said."

"I *do* remember what the doctor said. You don't have to remind me. Please understand that this baby—" she placed her hand gently on her stomach "—is the most important thing in the world to me. *Everything* I do will be in its best interests!"

Matt mulled over her words as he drove to Molly's place.

And they gave him a feeling of hope. If Liz truly meant what she'd said, then she would agree to put off any court action till after her baby was born, because avoiding that conflict would be in the baby's best interests.

In a lighter mood he parked in front of Molly's and it was with a jaunty step that he walked up her front path.

She opened the door before he could knock.

"Hi!" Her hazel eyes sparkled as she came out. Dancing past him onto the path, she twirled around. "How do you like my new dress? Isn't it pretty?"

It was, he thought, as she looked up at him eagerly.

And the bronze color brought out the topaz flecks in her eyes...

But the only eyes he could think about were Liz's— and the lonely expression he'd seen in them when he'd popped out to the patio to tell her he was leaving. With all his heart, he'd wished he could have canceled this evening with Molly and spent it with—

"*Well?*" Molly prodded.

"You look terrific," he said, trying to inject warm enthusiasm into his voice. "The dress is perfect on you."

She made a dainty curtsy. "Thank you, kind sir. And you, may I say, look fantastic!"

"Well, thank *you!*" He cupped her elbow and led her down the path. "New perfume, too?"

"Mmm." Her voice was husky as she went on, "Tonight's special...so I decided to splurge."

"Where are the kids?"

"Mrs. Bertuzzi's baby-sitting, and..."

She paused and he sensed an odd fluttering tension in the air.

"And?" he prompted, opening the car door for her.

Her cheeks were pink, her eyes coyly lowered. "And—" as she slipped by him her breasts brushed his arm "—I've arranged for them to sleep over. At her place."

"Sounds like a good idea," Matt said absently, before he slammed the door.

It wasn't till he was rounding the trunk that a dismaying thought stopped him short. And he felt a stab of alarm as he put two and two and two together.

First there was Molly's husky "Tonight's special," then the new dress, the new perfume, the coy blush, the brushing of her breasts against his arm...and finally...her arrangement to have the kids sleep over at the baby-sitter's.

Was she setting the stage for *seduction?*

The thought appalled him.

He'd never seen Molly as anything but the wife, and then the widow, of his old buddy Dave; and he had never said or done anything to lead her to think of him as anything more than a reliable friend. But somewhere along the way she must have got the wrong idea, and she'd fantasized their relationship into something more.

He struggled with a growing feeling of horror as he opened the door on the driver's side.

How the *heck* was he going to get himself out of this!

In the end, his worries were for naught—at least temporarily—because by the evening's end, everything had unraveled.

Just before the last dance the emcee came looking for them, to tell Molly she had a phone call. The caller was Mrs. Bertuzzi, the boys' baby-sitter.

Matt stood by as Molly took the call, and when she put the phone down, she looked distressed.

"It's Iain," she said. "He's got a fever and he's been really sick and he wants to go home." Her eyes shimmered with disappointment. "I'm sorry, Matt. We'll have to leave."

When they got to Mrs. Bertuzzi's, the baby-sitter had the children waiting. Iain was glassy-eyed and flushed.

No sooner did they get him home, than he was sick again.

Molly told Matt he should go on home, but Iain cried that he wanted his uncle Matt to stay.

So Matt stayed.

Molly put the boys to bed, and though Stuart went to sleep right away, Iain was weepy and still feeling very sick. He wanted Matt to sit by his bed, so Matt did. And it wasn't till almost four o'clock that the child's stomach finally settled, and he drifted into a deep sleep.

Matt got up from his chair and stretched.

"Thanks so much for staying." Molly wiped back a wisp of damp hair from her forehead and then said, ruefully, as she glanced down at her crumpled dress, "Well, this evening didn't turn out quite as I'd planned, but then with kids in the picture, things rarely do! I'm sorry I've kept you up so late—I'll have to make it up to you another time."

Before then, Matt thought as she saw him out, he'd have to find a moment to tell her—in as gentle a way as possible—that although he valued her as a friend, he'd never see her as anything more.

Liz woke suddenly, not sure what had disturbed her.

But she needed to go to the bathroom.

She rolled out of bed, and was almost at the door when she heard the sound of a car outside.

She changed direction and padded over to the window. Cautiously parting the slats of the venetian miniblinds, she peered down. And was just in time to see Matt striding from his Taurus, the white moonlight creating a long, thin shadow that glided behind him as he walked to the house.

She'd assumed that he had come home hours ago.

Instead he'd been out with Molly till—she glanced at the clock—after four!

She felt a sinking sensation deep in the pit of her stomach—and then was furious with herself. Why should the fact that Matt and Molly had been having sex upset her—because of course they'd been having sex. Two mature adults on the brink of becoming engaged didn't go dancing and then stay up half the night playing tiddledywinks!

She slumped against the wall, and stayed there till after she heard Matt come upstairs and go into his room.

Then she waited till he'd had time to fall asleep, so she could creep through to the bathroom undetected.

The last thing she wanted was for him to know that she'd been awake when he came home. It was bad enough that she had to picture him making love to Molly, but if he heard her moving around and came out to investigate, he might sense her misery and might guess what had caused it.

If he knew how she felt about him, it would make life very awkward. Humiliating for her; embarrassing for him. She would have to find some way of making sure he believed she no longer had any feelings for him.

And she should do it at the very first opportunity.

When she went downstairs in the morning, Matt had already left for the office.

The kitchen was empty but he must have cooked bacon and eggs for himself—the smell still lingered in the air and when she opened the dishwasher to insert her juice glass, she saw a plate with a trace of eggs on the surface.

He had left her a note on the table.

I'll Be Home At Noon. Have Your Answer Ready.

"Oh, yes, I'll have my answer ready," she murmured. "And it's going to be the same *no* as I gave you last night!"

But even as she tossed the note into the garbage, the lingering smell of fried food suddenly got to her and she felt queasy. Her stomach started to roll...

She hurried out of the kitchen and ran upstairs to the bathroom and got there just in time.

She was even more violently sick than she'd been yesterday.

And by the time she emerged from the bathroom, she didn't have the strength to do anything but crawl back to bed.

And that's where Matt found her, when he came home.

She woke to the sound of his *rat-tat* on her half-open bedroom door.

Raising heavy eyelids, she watched him come over to the bed...and the expression on his face was grim.

"For heaven's sake, Liz, what's going on? Why are you in bed? Aren't you feeling well? Did you—"

"Matt." Weakly she put up a hand to halt him. "Don't harangue me. I didn't *do* anything. I got up after you'd gone, and I went downstairs, but I felt sick, then after, I felt groggy so I decided to lie down. I guess I fell asleep again."

His mouth compressed into a thin line; and his voice, when he finally spoke, was rough with emotion.

"That's it, Liz. From now on, you do as I say. No 'ifs, ands or buts.' Until this baby is safely delivered, you and I will live here, together, as amicably as we can.''

As Liz opened her mouth to respond, he drowned her out.

''For heaven's sake, woman, you don't have the energy to look after your*self,* how do you expect to survive if you insist on getting involved in a fight for this property—''

''Stop!'' Shakily Liz pushed herself up on one elbow. ''You're right. I give in. I'm not going to let pride get in the way of doing what's best for this baby. Yes, I'll agree with your plan. We'll live here together, for the time being, because I don't have the strength to shove you out and I don't have the will to go find somewhere else to live. So—'' she fell back on her pillows ''—let's call a truce. Till after the baby is born. And then—'' she took in a deep breath ''—it'll be a fight to the finish, no holds barred.''

He had won.

Matt could barely hide his satisfaction. The only thing that kept him from dancing one of his mother's Scottish jigs was the sight of Liz's pale pinched face.

So instead of showing his delight, he sat down on the edge of the bed, and rested a hand lightly on her hip.

''Could you eat something now?'' he asked. ''I think I could rustle up some chicken soup, a few crackers...''

''That would be great. Thanks.'' She put a casual hand atop his, just for a second, before withdrawing it again. ''You're being very kind. I appreciate it. I have to admit,'' she added, ''that I was nervous, before I came back home, about the possibility of meeting up with you again.''

''You had no reason to be nervous of me.''

''Oh, I know that now...but...the truth is, I was afraid I might still be attracted to you. I tell you—'' she wrinkled her nose ''—it's been an enormous relief to find that whatever I felt for you before was merely teenage infatuation...and it's totally gone.'' She closed her eyes, and a rueful sigh whispered from between her lips. ''It was nice, of course, at the time. But it's even nicer that it's over. I wouldn't *ever* want to ride that roller coaster of emotions again!''

She might as well have kicked him in the crotch with a pointy-toed stiletto. It would have been less painful.

And as he walked downstairs a few moments later, he reflected self-derisively that, like Molly, he had built himself a fantasy world. A fantasy world in which he and Liz would end up together...and live happily ever after.

He'd realized it might take a long time to regain her trust, but he'd managed to convince himself he could eventually do it.

He hadn't even considered the possibility that she no longer had any interest in him.

But that didn't change the way he felt about her— the way he had always felt about her. That would never change. And he would look after her for as long as she needed him.

He would just have to make sure she never found out that he was still in love with her, because if she ever did, it would make life very awkward. Humiliating for him; and very embarrassing for her.

*   *   *

After Matt left the bedroom, Liz got up. She smoothed down her shirt and slacks, and went through to the bathroom to freshen up before going downstairs.

When she entered the kitchen, Matt was setting a bowl of soup on a small tray.

"You don't have to bring that upstairs," she said, as he looked around. "I'm feeling better. Mmm, that smells good." She threw him a friendly smile. "Out of a can?"

"Out of the freezer."

"Ah. From Molly...or your mom?"

"My mother. She makes the best chicken soup... and she believes it's a cure for whatever ails you."

"You're going to have some, too?"

"No, I've arranged to have lunch with a client...I was planning to go right back to the office."

"Do you have to rush? I have a few questions to ask, they've been niggling at me."

"Sure, I have a minute or two."

He set her soup bowl and cutlery on the table, along with a plate of crackers, a napkin and a dish of butter. Pulling out her chair, he waited for her to be seated, before leaning back against the counter and saying, "Okay, what did you want to know?"

She picked up her soup spoon. "When I phoned here a couple of weeks ago from New York—"

"You called? But you didn't leave a message."

"I didn't call to *talk* to anyone, I just called because I wanted to make sure my father was still here. And when I heard his voice on the answering machine...of course I assumed he was. So what I was wondering was why—'

"Why his voice is still on the tape, and why didn't

I have that number disconnected when I moved in?''

She nodded. ''Why didn't you get your own new number, why don't you have your own message on the answering machine?''

''I did. And I do. The reason I didn't have the *old* line disconnected was…you didn't come home for your father's funeral so I assumed you didn't know he'd passed away. On the off chance that one day you would phone—which you eventually did—I was hoping I'd either be around to take your call or you would leave a message and your phone number, so I could call you back.''

''Oh, I see.''

''Would you have come home for the funeral, Liz, if you'd known—''

''Yes, of course.'' She sipped from her soup spoon, and swallowed before going on. ''But I wish now that I'd come back earlier, so I could have talked with my father before he died. I'd have dearly liked the chance to—''

''Mend fences. Yeah, it's really sad when that opportunity is missed.''

''Mend fences?'' She stared at him incredulously. ''You've got to be joking! I had no interest whatsoever in mending fences with my father. Mending fences implies that both sides were at fault. That's not the case here. If I did anything wrong, it was because I followed my heart. And my hormones,'' she added with a self-derisive laugh. ''Whereas my father…well, I believe that parents should love their children unconditionally. If my father ever loved me—and I'm not sure he ever did—he withdrew that love because I didn't live up to his standards. The only reason I wish I could have talked with him was so I could have told him—to his face—that that was *wrong*."

Matt frowned at her. "He wouldn't have been the man you remembered, Liz. And what good would it have done—"

"It might not have done *him* any good, but it would certainly have made *me* feel a whole lot better!"

He shook his head, as if he was disappointed in her. "The Liz I remember was compassionate—"

"That was another Liz. A different Liz." She pushed her soup bowl aside, her appetite gone, as smoldering old angers flared to brilliant new life. "We all have to be accountable for our actions, Matt. My father held me accountable for mine...no one ever held him accountable for his."

Matt made to speak but she overrode him. "And no one," she added bitterly, "ever held you accountable for yours."

She heard his shocked hiss of breath. "It took two, Liz."

"Yes, but you were twenty, a college student...while I was only seventeen, little more than a child."

"That," he said quietly, "was a low blow."

"You're a boxer," she retorted, "I'm sure you can handle it."

In a voice that held absolutely no intonation, he said, "I *was* a boxer, Liz. I no longer enjoy fighting."

"You said that you'd lost the heart for it. Maybe—" her own wounded heart made her want to draw blood from his "—what you lost was your nerve."

He remained silent and the stoniness of that silence only made her want to goad him further.

"I took you for many things." Her upper lip curled in distaste. "But a coward wasn't one of them."

If the atmosphere between them had been tense before, now it was so tight it almost choked her. She sensed that of all the things she might have accused him of, cowardice was the worst.

But he said nothing. He just kept looking at her, his expression now so sorrowful it made her want to weep. Tears of shame. Matt was right, it had indeed been a low blow to bring up their age difference. He had *never* taken advantage of her. In the beginning, he'd believed her to be older than she was; he hadn't known that as a gifted student she'd moved through school at an accelerated pace and had been ready to graduate at seventeen. By the time the misunderstanding had been sorted out, it was way too late; they were not only crazy about each other, but they had become lovers.

And there had been no going back.

"Liz, I know you'll never forgive me...but can't you find it in your heart to forgive your father?"

"Even if I could forgive him for his harsh treatment of me, I could never forgive him for betraying my mother. When he sold this house—"

"Liz, please let's not get into that again. Dammit, if I'd known we were going to get into this kind of discussion, I'd have gone right back to the office. It's not good for you...or the baby...when you get so upset!"

"It's not easy to stay calm when I think about what he did. This house was my *mother's*. It was in her family for four generations. He had no *right* to sell it! He had no right to sell my memories! Everywhere I look, I'm reminded of Mom, of the things we did together, the happy times we shared. How could he have—'' She broke off, and he saw she was close to tears. But she clenched her jaw and said stubbornly, ''Nothing you can say will ever make me feel any differently about him.''

There *was* something he could say that might make a difference—something he'd been told in confidence. But he was willing to break that confidence if it would help Liz to forgive her father. And he would talk to Gavin later, explain what he had done and why. Gavin would understand.

''Liz, there's something you don't know. About your father.''

''Nothing you can say will change how I—''

''Hear me out.'' He pulled back his chair a little and set his hands on his thighs. ''Liz, you *did* try to contact your father, didn't you…six or seven years ago?''

''How…how on earth did you know that?''

''You phoned him several times, you even left a number where you could be reached. Is that right?''

Numbly she nodded.

''But your father didn't pick up the phone…and he never called you back.''

''If you're going to say that he couldn't, because of his stroke—''

''I'm not going to say that. His speech was badly impaired, but he *was* able to communicate, through sounds and gestures, with one person—his attendant, the male nurse who looked after him. So—''

''So he could have had this nurse talk to me. He didn't. He *chose* not to,'' she added scornfully.

''He chose not to because he believed that if you found out he was incapacitated, you would have come home to look after him. He knew the kind of person you were, Liz, and he didn't want to be a burden to you. *Not* contacting you was probably the most unselfish thing your father ever did.''

Her face had become pale. "How can you *possibly* know this?"

"Gavin Smythe—your father's nurse—has been a friend of mine for the past few years. He'd looked after your father at Laurel House from the time he had his stroke, so after your father died, I asked Gavin if you were coming home for the funeral. He said nobody knew where you were…and that's when he told me about those old calls. He'd kept a note of the number, and he tried to track you down that way but the woman it had belonged to—a Melissa Brent—had passed away seven years ago and after that, the trail went cold. Who was she, Liz?"

"An old friend of my mother's who lived in Chicago."

"That's where you went, after you ran away?"

"Yes, I contacted Melissa, and she took me in, looked after me, eventually put me through college. She'd never married, and she had no family of her own so she more or less adopted me. When she died, I was devastated, and I felt…lost. And for the first time, I thought about going home. But when my father didn't return my calls, I figured nothing had changed so I shut him out of my mind. I moved to New York, made a fresh start. And I built myself a successful career and had a good life there."

"Which is what your father wanted for you."

"If what Gavin Smythe told you is true, then yes, that *is* what he wanted for me. But that still doesn't excuse him for betraying my mother. She owned

Laurel House when she married him, Matt...but she put his name on the deed, too. Then years later, when she knew she was dying, she made him promise that when I was twenty-one, he'd put my name on the deed along with his own. It's clear he didn't do that, or he couldn't have sold the house without my agreement.'' She sighed. ''Let's drop it, shall we? We're never going to agree on who should really have possession of this house!''

He was more than happy to drop it; the last thing he wanted was to upset her by arguing.

''Sure.'' He got up. ''I should be on my way now anyway. Is there anything I can pick up for you in town?''

She rose from her chair. ''How about a can of gas for my car?''

The mocking humor in her tone made him smile.

''Good try...but no, you're to take it easy till your next visit to the doc and that means no driving. Anything you need—other than gas!—give me a call and I'll pick it up for you.''

He felt like a husband. He wished he *were* her husband. He'd give anything to pick up the phone at work and hear her say, ''Darling, could you bring home a pint of milk?''

She walked him to the door, and as she hovered there, with the sunlight sparkling in her silky blond hair, he was sorely tempted to kiss her goodbye. Which he would have done, had he been her husband.

But he wasn't.

So he didn't.

CHAPTER SEVEN

THE following days passed quietly for Liz.

She had always loved country life and she relished the peace she found at Laurel House—and especially enjoyed the warm afternoons spent out-of-doors, when she would lie on a chaise in the shade, and dream dreams of her coming baby.

She and Matt had settled into a routine that was casual and comfortable on the surface. But underneath there shimmered a constant sexual tension, and Liz did her best to avoid any physical contact with him because even the merest brushing of his shoulder against hers could set explosions of sensation dancing across her skin.

It might have been easier if they hadn't been alone together so much, but their only visitor was Naomi, and most often she came by during the day—she worked evening shifts as housekeeper at Sandford's Inn, and was kept busy between times in her position as Tradition's assistant mayor.

Liz liked Matt's mother, and the older woman seemed to like her, too. Although Naomi always had a purpose when she came—usually to vacuum, garden, or deliver a casserole—she invariably took time to sit and share a pot of peppermint tea with Liz, before scooting away on her bicycle.

And it was on one such visit that she mentioned to Liz that Molly had been down with flu.

"The boys had it first," she said, as Liz reached

over the patio table to refill her teacup. "And then Molly got it. She's up and about again, and when I talked to her yesterday, she said to let you know she'd be in touch soon." Naomi sat back in her chair. "And how are *you* feeling? When do you see Dr. Black for your next checkup?"

"Tomorrow. I'm feeling really well. The morning sickness has passed, thank goodness. And Matt has been doing such a good job of looking after me—he's treating me as if I were made of Waterford crystal!"

"Just enjoy it." Naomi's eyes were warm with affection. "Being pregnant is a special time in a woman's life, and you have always been very special to Matt."

Oh, sure, Liz mused cynically; she'd always been very special to him...so special that when she'd told him thirteen years ago that she was pregnant with his child he'd looked at her as if she'd sprouted three extra heads.

"Liz?" Naomi's tone was questioning. "Does it *bother* you that Matt wants to look after you?"

Liz liked the other woman too much to lie to her. "What bothers me is that he seems to think that if he looks after me this time around, it'll make up for his rejection of me when I was expecting *his* child. It won't. He should have been there to support me through what was a very difficult pregnancy; he should have been there to share the sorrow when our baby was stillborn. Instead he took all the pleasure, suffered none of the pain. He walked away, Naomi. He got off scot-free."

"Oh, no, Liz, he—" Naomi gulped back whatever she'd been going to say, and clamped her lips together as if to stop the words from gushing out by themselves. She gazed entreatingly at Liz, as if asking for something.

But asking for what? Understanding? But Liz didn't understand. Couldn't understand, unless Matt's mother explained.

"Naomi?"

Naomi shook her head. "Please forget what I said."

"But you didn't say anything!"

"I'm sorry." Obviously distressed, Naomi added, "I can't say anymore. But...I would ask you one thing, Liz. Please...will you try not to be too hard on Matt? You really *are* very special to him and always have been. It took years for him to get over losing you. And I sometimes wonder if he ever did."

"He didn't *lose* me. He...made his choice...and he chose—"

"He panicked," Naomi said softly. "And in that moment of initial panic, he thought he had to make a choice...and in not wanting to hurt me, he ended up hurting you."

"But...how could he have hurt *you?*"

"I said he *thought* he had to make a choice."

"I don't understand..."

"Let me explain. When Matt's father died, I was left with a six-year-old to bring up alone. I had no money, no training. I took two jobs—waitressing and housecleaning—and saved every penny I could to put money by for Matt's education. As soon as he was old enough to work after school he did, every chance he got. His dream was to study law, and my only goal was to help him achieve that dream. Together, we were going to make it happen. Then...he was just beginning his third year when you told him you were pregnant. He knew he couldn't support you unless he—"

"Unless he dropped out and got a job. I know that, Naomi, and I know it would have been a sacrifice to give up his dreams but in life there are consequences—"

"Matt wasn't thinking of himself, Liz, he was thinking of me. Of the sacrifices he believed *I* had made, for him. What he didn't realize was that I never looked on it that way, everything I did for him I did out of love. All I wanted was to see him happy. If he hadn't panicked, if he'd brought you to me instead...we'd have somehow managed. We would have been a *family*."

Liz's throat suddenly felt painfully constricted. She swallowed, but when she spoke, her voice still came out huskily.

"I wish...that could have happened. I never really had that kind of family...not after my mother died. My father...well, he didn't know much about bringing up children."

"Your father wasn't an easy man, Liz. But I'm sure he did love you...in his own way."

When Matt's mother left about ten minutes later, Liz stood at the front door watching her cycle away.

Leaning against the doorjamb, she let her thoughts drift back to their conversation...and in particular, to Naomi's protesting "Oh, no!" after Liz had said Matt had got off scot-free. What had his mother been about to say before she cut herself off? Whatever it was, she had seemed *really* upset. But about what? No matter how Liz tried to come up with some answer, an explanation eluded her.

Eventually she went inside and as she crossed the

foyer, she felt the waistband of her shorts digging into her stomach. Unfastening the button to relieve the pressure, she reflected that *all* her waistbands were beginning to feel too tight. She needed to go shopping for maternity clothes.

But Matt still hadn't put gas in her car. He'd made no secret of his reason: he wanted to control her movements, keep her from doing too much.

But she was feeling a lot better now. Maybe tomorrow, after she saw the doctor, she could do some shopping.

She went through to the kitchen and phoned Matt's office. Frannie put her through right away.

"What's wrong?" Matt's tone was sharp with concern.

"Nothing's wrong," Liz said with exaggerated patience. "I'm just calling to ask you to bring home a can of gas tonight for my car."

"Why?"

"I want to go shopping tomorrow for maternity clothes."

"I'll drive you."

"Matt, it's not necessary for you to take time off work. I know how busy you are. If you don't bring home gas, I'll walk into town and carry a can home myself!"

"No way! Tell you what, Liz. Today's Thursday, the Sagebrush Mall and most of the other stores in Crestville are open tonight till nine. I'll come home early, we'll have a leisurely drive there, have a nice dinner out and then I'll poke around in a bookstore while you do your shopping."

Before she could argue, he added in a pathetic mock-whine, "I need the break, Miz Rossiter. I bin cookin' and slavin' for you for weeks, don't I deserve a night out?''

Liz chuckled, but said, "Matt, I really am able to drive myself around. I don't need any more cosseting!''

"I'll make a deal." His voice had reverted to its usual baritone. "If you let me drive you to Crestville tonight, we'll drop by the gas station tomorrow after you visit the doc, and then you'll be mobile again."

She could see he wasn't about to give in; and it was tempting to have someone else do the driving.

"All right," she said. "You've got yourself a deal."

"Great. Now don't forget to have a nap this afternoon, and I'll be by to pick you up around four-thirty."

Liz was about to go upstairs around two for her nap, when someone rang the front door bell.

She crossed the foyer and opened the door, to find Molly standing there. Looking trim and attractive in blue jeans and a navy T-shirt, the perky brunette beamed at her.

"Hi, there, Beth—oops!" Molly laughed. "Liz!" She gave Liz a hug, enveloping her in her light floral perfume.

"Molly, come in! Are you feeling better?"

"Right as rain." Molly walked into the foyer. "But how about you? I believe you're expecting a happy event!"

Naomi had told Liz days ago that her pregnancy was now common knowledge in town.

"Not that Matt or I spilled the beans," she'd confided, "but Matt's receptionist, Frannie, is a chum of

Molly's and when Frannie told Molly you'd fainted in Matt's office, it apparently confirmed what Molly had already guessed—her having been a nurse—and Molly said as much to Frannie. And though Frannie's the soul of discretion when it comes to her work, when it comes to local gossip…well, her lips are a wee bit loose.''

"I'm feeling fine," Liz said now to Molly. "Better every day!" She gestured toward the sitting room. "Let's go in here. Can I offer you a cup of tea? Coffee?"

"No, thanks," Molly said as they wandered into the room. "I just had lunch." She dropped into a tub chair and looked rather wistfully across at Liz who had perched on a sofa. "There's nothing quite like that first pregnancy. I envy you, because it's all so…new. You have so much to look forward to…have you felt the baby move yet?"

"Yes, I have."

"Isn't it thrilling, the first time you notice it? But the first time for everything's exciting, whereas in the second pregnancy, it's almost old hat. I'd always wanted a big family," Molly burbled on. "Do you remember that? When we were kids, we used to tell each other all our secrets."

"Mmm. You thought four was the perfect number."

"I still do! And…I know Matt loves kids. He's been like a dad to Iain and Stuart since Dave died." Molly's hazel eyes glowed. "Oh, I just feel I can still confide in you, Liz, it's as if all those years between had just melted away. I just can't tell you how wonderful it is to have found a man like Matt. I thought—when Dave died—that I'd never want to be with anyone else…but now…"

"I'm happy for you, Molly." Liz was astounded that she managed to sound so calm. "And for Matt, too."

"Honey, are you *sure* you're feeling okay? You look awfully pale. Oh, I'm so selfish, going on and on about how wonderful everything is for me...and never even asking you about your baby's father. Is he...will he be coming here, to Tradition?"

"No. I'm on my own, Molly."

"Do you want to talk about it?"

"There's nothing to say, really. Colin didn't want this baby. We'd been together for five years and we parted amicably enough...I stayed on for a while to tie up all the loose ends and then...I came home, to make a new life here."

"I hope it works out for you." Molly got to her feet. "Listen, honey, you do look tired. I'm going to go now, let you have a nap. You do have a nap every afternoon, don't you? It's very important."

"Yes, I do." Liz got up, too.

She walked Molly to the front door. And as they stood on the stoop, Molly said, "I'm so glad you came back, Liz. I know we're going to be *great* friends again. And while it's good of Matt to let you stay on here till you're feeling stronger, once you move out I hope you find a nice place not too far from Laurel House, so that we'll find it easy to visit each other whenever we feel like it."

So Matt hadn't told Molly about her own claim to Laurel House. It would surely jolt her...just as it now jolted Liz to realize that Molly was of course planning on living here with Matt. As his wife. Liz hadn't thought that far ahead.

"Oh!" Molly clapped a hand to her forehead. "I

almost forgot the reason I came up to see you! I wanted to invite you for dinner tomorrow evening. I'm going to try out a new lasagna recipe…and I'd like you to meet my boys.''

Liz didn't really want to go, it was hard to put on a happy face when Molly spoke about herself and Matt—but how could she refuse without being rude?

''That would be lovely, Molly. What time?''

''Around five.''

''Where do you live?''

''You don't have to worry about that.'' Molly patted Liz's arm and then sauntered away toward her car.

''Why not?''

''Matt knows where I live,'' she called back gaily. ''Heavens, he spends half his time at my place! He's coming, too…you can drive over together.''

As Molly drove away, Liz stared frustratedly after the car. The last thing she wanted was to spend an evening with Matt and Molly, watching them bill and coo over each other.

But now she had committed herself to it.

Matt got home at twenty after four.

The house felt empty. He strode across the foyer, calling out, ''Liz?'' but no one answered.

About to go upstairs, he heard the patio door opening. He crossed to the sitting room and saw Liz coming in from outside. She was wearing a cream silk shirt over slim black pants, and with her flaxen hair cascading sleekly over her shoulders, she looked so beautiful it made his heart ache.

''Hi,'' he said. ''I was just about to go upstairs and look for you—I thought you might have overslept.''

"Sorry—I did hear the car arrive, but I was down at the foot of the garden."

"You look fantastic."

Blushing, she said in a flustered voice, "Thanks. I didn't know where you were taking me for dinner but I assumed it wouldn't be McDonald's or the food fair at the mall, and these slacks were the only dressy ones I could fit into...and even these wouldn't meet at the waist so I've had to fasten them with a safety pin—"

"Aw, rats," he teased, "there goes the image!"

She laughed. And he was glad to see her relax.

"So," he said, "you're ready to leave?"

She nodded.

"Okay." He ran a hand over his jaw, felt it sandpaper rough. "Give me a couple of minutes to freshen up."

As he stood in the bathroom scraping a razor over his jaw, his high spirits over this outing with Liz reminded him of the way he used to feel thirteen years ago when he'd been getting ready for one of their secret trysts. He'd always been dizzy with impatience but still he'd taken the time to shave carefully first so his jaw wouldn't rasp her skin. He knew Liz's father would notice if her cheeks were grazed and he didn't want to alert him to the fact that his daughter had a boyfriend. Not that he'd been afraid of the man. Although Max Rossiter had been six foot three and built like a bull, Matt knew that with his own boxing skills he could have danced rings around the guy. But he'd been afraid for Beth, who couldn't stand up to her father's rages.

He finished shaving...and smiled cynically as he regarded his rugged reflection in the mirror. He was no oil painting. But for some odd reason, women still found him attractive.

Except for the one woman he wanted.

She had told him point-blank that he left her cold.

He wasn't about to give up, though.

"Faint heart never won fair lady."

Whoever had said that first had got it right and from now on, it would be his mantra.

"What a charming place!" Liz said, as Matt drew the Taurus up in the graveled forecourt of the Cedars Inn, which was situated on the outskirts of Crestville.

The off-white and slate-blue building was set high above a lake, in acres of emerald lawn adorned by beds of peach and tangerine roses. Along a sloping path to the east of the entrance, on a knoll, stood a rustic wishing well.

"Yeah," Matt said, "it's nice. Food's great, too."

They strolled to the front door, but as Matt pulled it open a knot of people came toward them from inside, and putting a protective arm around Liz's shoulders, he held her back, while keeping the door open for the oncoming group.

She was pressed against him for not more than twenty seconds, but it was long enough for her to become excruciatingly aware of the possessive strength of his hard-muscled arm and the intimate pressure of his hip against her thigh. A wave of wanting made her knees weak. She yearned to slide her arms around his waist, lean her cheek against his heart, inhale his heady male scent...

But if she did, would she also smell Molly's distinctive floral perfume on his shirt—just as she'd smelled the faint memory of it lingering in his car?

The thought acted like a bucket of icy water, dousing the flame of desire that had licked through her. For a moment there she'd let her guard down, had forgotten about the hurts of the past; had forgotten, too, that Matt was spoken for. She'd been enjoying his company; now she felt all her pleasure fade.

And the moment Matt released her, she stepped quickly away from him and walked into the foyer, trying to put as much distance between them as possible.

The maître d' seated them at a window table overlooking the lake. And though she'd have given anything to be sitting at home, alone, she nevertheless put on her brightest smile and pretended to be having a good time.

Their conversation rolled easily over dinner—she asked him about local people she'd known when she was growing up and Matt filled her in, where he could, on what had happened to them. But when they reached the coffee stage, she noticed that he seemed distracted.

"Penny for them!" she said, and saw him start. "Or are they worth more?" she teased.

He gazed at her consideringly for a few moments, and then he said, "I don't know what they're worth, but *you* do."

She raised her eyebrows.

"I was actually thinking," he said slowly, "about the man you left behind in New York. And I was wondering how you feel about him now."

She stiffened, but before she could say anything, he said bluntly,

"Are you still in love with him?"

"Love isn't like water in a tap, Matt." She tried to

sound faintly amused. "You can't just turn it on and off at will."

"So you're still in love with the guy."

"Excuse me—" the waiter hovered at their table "—would either of you like some more coffee?"

Liz shook her head. "Not for me, thanks."

Matt said, "No, we're finished"

"I'll bring your bill, then." The waiter headed toward the back of the restaurant.

"Liz—"

"Matt, the evening's wearing on and I'd really like to get to the stores. If you'll excuse me, I'll just pop through to the ladies' first." She pushed back her chair. "I'll meet you outside."

"You're running away."

She rose to her feet. He did, too.

"No, Matt, you've got me confused with Beth. Liz Rossiter doesn't run." She squared her shoulders. "The answer to your question is yes, I still love Colin."

She thought his eyes darkened, but she didn't give him a chance to respond. "I'll probably always love him," she said, "because of what we had together and because he's the father of my child. We were together for five years, and I think about him often, I still shed tears because we *had* something special and we lost it. But I'm no longer *in love* with him. He wasn't quite the man I'd thought he was."

She turned away then and threaded her way between the tables. When she got to the ladies' room, she was thankful to find it deserted. She stood at the sink, her breath coming fast, as she stared distraughtly at her reflection in the mirror.

To her surprise she looked just as neatly groomed

as she had when she and Matt had left the house—
she'd half expected to look as if she'd been in a cy-
clone. That was the way she felt, with her heart and
mind all blown around and topsy-turvy.

Why had she told Matt she was no longer in love
with Colin? Couldn't she have lied about that? Then
perhaps, if he believed her heart belonged to another,
he would stop gazing at her the way he'd been doing
a few moments ago...as if he wanted her more than
life itself.

He was standing at the wishing well when she went
outside.

She walked up the path to join him. A soft breeze
gusted from the lake, and she put up a hand to hold
back her hair as it blew over her face. It was a perfect
evening—and very like the June evening when she and
Matt had first met, at a rock concert in Elwood Park.

The bittersweet memory of that precious evening
tugged at her heartstrings, and made her throat ache
painfully. They had been so sure then that they were
made for each other. Kindred spirits. Soul mates.

"Here." Matt held out a shiny quarter as she
reached him. "Make a wish."

She dragged herself out of the swamp of nostalgia.
No good would come of dwelling on the past; that
part of her life was over. Over and done with. She had
come back to Tradition to move forward, not to drift
back.

She took the quarter and as she did, her fingertips
brushed the pad of his thumb and she felt a tingle of
sensation run up her arm.

She ignored it and stepped to the opposite side of

the well. Looking across at him, she said, lightly, "How about you? Aren't you going to make one?"

"I already have."

"What did you wish for?"

"That would be telling." His mouth curved in a lazy smile. "But if it comes true," he said, "you'll know it." He gestured toward the well. "Go ahead."

What did he mean, she would "know it"? Perhaps he hadn't actually proposed to Molly yet; but when he did, Liz would certainly know it because the air would be abuzz with wedding plans.

So...what should *she* wish for?

She *could* have wished for Matt's love. But he had proved in the past that she couldn't trust him...and love without trust was a useless thing.

And even if, by some miracle, she *could* have trusted him again, it was too late. He was Molly's now. Molly's fingerprints were all over him. Her underwear was in his house. Her scent was in his car. Her heart was in his hands.

Liz dropped the quarter into the well and as it hit the water below with a tiny splash, she closed her eyes.

And wished for what she wanted most in all the world:

A happy, healthy full-term baby.

CHAPTER EIGHT

Liz and Matt split up when they reached the mall and Liz soon found Stork Feathers, a maternity clothing store jam-packed with attractive outfits.

When she'd finished shopping, she walked along to the Bay to browse in their Baby Department as she still had some time remaining before she was to meet Matt.

She'd just picked up two packages of infant-size sleepers and had moved on to admire a crib decorated with Disney decals, when she felt someone touch her shoulder.

Turning, she found Matt right behind her.

"Hi," he said. "I saw you pass the bookstore and decided to follow you in case you were done." He glanced down at her pink-and-blue striped carrier bags with their stork logo. "Find what you were looking for?"

"Mmm. How about you?"

"I got a couple of books." He indicated a glossy blue bag swinging from his hand.

"Are you ready to leave now?"

"Yeah." He reached up to touch a mobile suspended over the crib, and the zebras, giraffes and lions bobbed smoothly up and down. "Hey," he said with a chuckle, "cool!"

She looked at his laughing upturned face, and it hit her like a slap that this was how it should have been, thirteen years ago. The two of them, in a Baby

Department somewhere, looking at baby things... together.

It stung, that he should be here with her now, and pushing himself in where she didn't want him to be. She was having this baby on her own, he was the last person from whom she'd accept any help, advice, or support!

She felt overwhelmed by hurtful memories. "I'm ready to leave, too," she said. "I just have to pay for a couple of items."

"Sure." He tipped the mobile again. And chuckled again. "Go ahead."

She stalked away toward the nearest Service Center, resentment making her head pound.

"What cute sleepers!" the clerk said as she took Liz's credit card. "A gift? Would you like a box?"

"No, thanks, they're for myself."

"Oh, lovely! When's the baby due?"

"Not till the end of the year."

"So you have lots of time to get everything ready." The woman rang up the sale. "Boy or a girl?"

"I don't know...don't want to, really."

"Then you're wise buying yellow, can't go wrong!"

"It's one of my favorite colors. I plan on having the baby's room yellow and white."

"That'll be nice and fresh. And besides—" the clerk returned the credit card "—if your next baby's not the same sex as the first, you won't need to re-decorate the nursery!"

Liz murmured something noncommittal, and stuffed her credit card back into her wallet. As she did, some-one behind her slid a gaily colored box across the counter.

"I'll have this," he said. "Thanks."

It was Matt.

And the box contained a mobile similar to the one he'd been admiring.

When he saw her quick frown, he spread out his hands in a gesture of mock-helplessness. "So sue me," he drawled. "I couldn't resist."

"This is for me?" Her voice was cool with disapproval.

"Not for you." His smile made crinkles fan out from his laughing eyes. "Not for you. For your baby."

I don't want you buying stuff for my baby!

She bit back the words, because she didn't want to be ungracious, and restricted herself to saying, "You shouldn't have. You've already bought me a beautiful meal."

He waved her words aside. And after he'd completed his purchase, he escorted her back to the car, where he tossed all their packages into the back seat.

As they drove out of the car park, he said, "Tired?"

"Mmm. But it's common, in pregnancy, to be tired in the evenings. I have to admit that I wouldn't be up to doing this every night!"

"Ah well, tomorrow night you'll have the house to yourself, you can have your supper on a tray, put your feet up and relax. I'm going out."

"To Molly's. Yes, I know." When Matt turned to look at her, his expression was questioning. "She invited me for dinner, too. I didn't know," she added, "when I accepted the invitation, that she'd already invited you."

A look of annoyance flitted over his face. It was quite obvious that he didn't want her there. And it hurt. But if he didn't want her there, she wanted it even less.

"I'm sorry." Her voice came out stiltedly. "As I said, if I'd known you were already invited I—"

"It's not your fault." His hands tightened around the steering wheel. "It's just that I haven't seen Molly for the past couple of weeks as she and the family have been coping with flu, but…there was something important I planned to talk with her about tomorrow evening, and now—"

"I'll call her. I'll make up some excuse and—"

"No." He shook his head. "As I said, it's important, but it can wait."

"Matt, I—"

"Forget it." He had become detached. "We'll go over there tomorrow evening for dinner, as arranged. You'll have a good time, you'll enjoy meeting Iain and Stuart. They're great kids. I love them as if they were my own."

But they weren't his own, Liz reflected unhappily. The child that *would* have been his own would have been twelve years old now. The baby had been a girl. The doctors had told her that much.

Liz sighed as a wave of sorrow swept over her. Not a day passed that she didn't think about her little daughter. Not a day passed that she didn't shed a tear over her. She had thought, at the time of her loss, that she would never get over it; she had thought that nothing would ever fill the aching void. But now she was expecting another baby, and this time everything would be all right.

Everything *had* to be all right.

She was counting on it.

Matt had slumped into silence, and she had no wish to break it.

When they arrived home, he opened the car door for her, and after she got out, he retrieved their packages from the back seat.

"How are you feeling now?" he asked, passing over her carrier bags as they walked into the house.

"Actually...I'm ready for bed."

"Can I bring you up something?" he asked, his tone solicitous. "A mug of hot chocolate? A couple of cookies?"

He sounded, she thought, like an "old married"; she half expected him to say, "Or how about a cup of tea, dear?" But he didn't *look* like an "old married"; he looked exactly what he was: dynamic and virile and more seductive than sin itself...and much more suited to getting *into* a woman's bed than setting a tray of tea and cookies on top of it!

"No, thanks." She made for the stairs. "I'll fall asleep, I think, the moment my head hits the pillow."

But as it turned out, she didn't, because when she got into bed she noticed that by mistake, Matt had given her his package, too, when they'd come into the house. It lay at the foot of her bed, along with her own unopened bags.

Had he bought a book he'd planned on reading tonight?

She scrambled down to the foot of the bed and hauled his package up. Then curious to see what his reading tastes were, she opened the glossy bag.

He had bought three books in all.

The first was the latest Grisham novel; but when she saw the other two, she stared in disbelief.

The first was: *A Handbook For The Mom-To-Be.*

The second was: *A Handbook For The Dad-To-Be.*

Resentment spread like brushfire through her veins. How *dare* he! Oh, it was bad enough that he'd taken it upon himself to buy *her* a baby book; but to take upon himself the role of father-in-waiting was—was—oh! she couldn't even come up with a word that was strong enough!

Throwing back her covers, she put on her robe, grabbed his bag of books and headed furiously out of her room.

Matt poked around the hall closet but came up with nothing.

What the devil had happened to his bag of books? Had he left them in the mall? Perhaps he'd left them on the—

He straightened and turned around when he heard footsteps thudding down the stairs.

He saw Liz come to an abrupt halt on the bottom step. She was pink-robed, and pink-cheeked, and she looked as if she was about to explode.

At him.

What the devil had he done now?

"I thought," he said, "you were going straight to b—"

He broke off abruptly as she held out a bag.

Uh-oh.

"These are yours," she snapped. "I brought them down, in case you wanted to read the Grisham book tonight."

The Grisham book wasn't the problem, neither was the mom-to-be book, which he'd planned to give her anyway.

But the other one—dammit, that one *was* a problem.

"Thanks." He walked over to take the bag but even as he grabbed it he felt the hostile vibes and backed quickly out of her space. "I did plan on starting the Grisham—"

She whirled around and started up the stairs again.

"Hold on," he called.

She stopped. But remained facing ahead. Her body was rigid.

He cleared his throat. "This one—" he took the mom's handbook from the bag "—I bought for you."

She turned then, and her cheeks were no longer pink but white.

"And the other?" She put a hand on the banister. "For yourself?"

He grimaced. "Yeah," he said in an apologetic voice. "Yeah, that one's for me. What I was planning was—"

"That the two of us would sit cozily of an evening, getting *ready for baby* together?"

The sarcasm in her tone cut him like a scalpel slash. "No. Not exactly. Actually I didn't mean you to see it. I planned to study it, find out how I could help you in the coming months. I didn't want you to go through this alone."

All of a sudden, the fire seemed to go out of her.

"Matt." Wearily she shook her head. "I *am* going to go through this alone. I want to go through it alone. And I am totally capable of going through it alone. So the best thing you can do is return that book, get your money back."

"Will you accept the one I bought for you? Unless, that is…maybe you already have enough baby books?"

"No," she said, grudgingly. "I don't have any. Not yet. I've been meaning to, but—"

"Then *will* you take it?"

Sighing, she said, "Matt, you really have to stop buying stuff for me."

"But you'll take it? *Please?*"

After a hesitation, she said quietly, "I suppose it would be churlish of me to refuse." She took the book when he handed it out to her, and clasped it over her chest. "Thank you." Unexpectedly she smiled. "It's kind of you."

He felt as if he were the one getting a gift. A smile from her was more precious to him than anything he could think of at that moment.

"So—" he smiled back at her "—friends again?"

Wry amusement twinkled in her eyes. "Friends," she said, "again! Good night, Matt."

"Sweet dreams."

He watched her as she walked up the stairs, her blond hair like a swathe of pale satin against her pink robe, and waited there till she disappeared across the landing.

Then he walked across the foyer and into his study, closing the door behind him before moving over to take a seat on his swivel chair. Leaning back, he set his feet on the desk, and from his plastic bag he drew out his new hardback copy of *A Handbook For The Dad-To-Be*.

Opening it at the beginning, he started to read.

Rain fell through the night, just enough to freshen the air and the countryside.

When Matt came back from his morning jog, he

found Liz outside, cutting white roses from a rambler by the door.

"Hi," he said, breathing hard, "great day, isn't it!"

"Mmm." She put a hand up to shade her eyes from the sun. "Do you jog every *single* morning?"

"Yup, like clockwork. How about you?" He ran lightly on the spot.

"No, I prefer to walk."

"Haven't seen you do much of that since you got here."

"No, I've been too nauseated in the mornings, then it's been too hot in the afternoons. But I know I *should* be walking."

She certainly should. That was one of the things he'd read in his baby book last night. "Early evening would be a good time," he said. "It's cooling off a bit by then."

"I suppose."

"Tell you what," he said, "we'll start taking a walk together after dinner. My workload's been strenuous lately and I find my stress builds up during the day. It would do me good, too, to get out and have a walk in the evening."

"We won't be able to walk *this* evening." She snipped one last delicate fragrant rose and turned toward the back door. "We'll be over at Molly's."

"That's no problem." He opened the door and stepped aside to let her walk by. "We can take the kids for a walk to the park after we eat dinner. Molly and I always do."

"Molly and I."

The casual way Matt had paired the two of them together stayed with Liz as she arranged the dainty roses in one of her mother's crystal bud vases; and it stayed with her for the rest of the day. It had sounded natural, and cozy.

And it gnawed at her heart like the tiny teeth of a field mouse. It also filled her with frustration—frustration with herself. She didn't want Matt, but yet she couldn't *stop* wanting him. And how mixed up was that! But she'd been mixed up about the man ever since she'd set eyes on him again. Her only hope was that once he was married, she'd be able to look at him without aching to be in his arms. And surely, once he was married, he'd stop looking at her as if he wanted exactly the same thing!

As they drove over to Molly's that evening, she could sense that he was in a bad mood. She snuck a peek at him and saw that his face was set in a brooding expression. He'd barely spoken a word to her since he'd come striding into the house half an hour ago.

All that he'd said then was, "Sorry I'm late. Client from hell. Meeting went on longer than I'd expected. Give me ten minutes..." And then he'd shot off upstairs.

When he'd come running down again, she was waiting in the front hall. He had showered and shaved and changed into a crisp white shirt and khaki chinos, but he still wore the harassed look he'd worn when he arrived home.

"Ready?" he'd said tersely, and without further ado had ushered her out to the car.

The drive to Molly's took ten minutes and during that time neither of them spoke. Only when he drew up in front of a cream stucco house did he say, unnecessarily, "Here we are."

"I can see," she said lightly, "that you are going to be charming company tonight."

About to open his car door, he paused, and looked around at her. "Sorry?"

She leveled a cool gaze at him. "I know you don't want me to be here. You couldn't have made that more plain. But the feeling is entirely mutual. Playing gooseberry isn't my idea of a fun night out! So—"

"Gooseberry?" He glowered at her. "What the hell are you talking about?"

She just melted every time she looked at him, and right now, she wondered if she had ever wanted him more. "I know," she said, her voice low, "that you and Molly are…"

"We're what?" he demanded. "Molly and I are…*what?*"

"Well—" she turned away from him and reached for her door handle "—I know that the two of you are going to be married."

The words had almost choked her. She fumbled for the handle but couldn't seem to find it. And as she wiped her forearm across her eyes, she felt him grab her wrist.

"Who the hell," he rasped, "told you that?"

Liz's breath caught as she stared into his fierce green eyes. He was obviously very angry with her…but she was even more angry with herself. She had jumped the gun, and she had been indiscreet. Sure, Molly had intimated that she and Matt were serious about each other, but no engagement had yet been announced. Perhaps Matt hadn't even got as far as proposing—and if he'd planned to do it tonight, which she'd surmised was his intention, he certainly wouldn't do it now, with her sitting there like a bump on a log.

"Matt, I—"

She didn't get a chance to go on because just then, her car door was opened from outside.

Matt released her wrist instantaneously, and drew back from her. Feeling dizzy, Liz turned toward the open door and saw Molly smiling down at her.

"Hi, there, we've all been waiting for you. It's great to see you, Liz! Come along inside."

Liz somehow managed to return Molly's smile and somehow managed to keep it in place as she got out of the car and stepped into Molly's welcoming hug.

"Sorry we're a bit late," Matt said, as he walked around the car to join them. "I got held up at the office."

"Oh, toot, that doesn't matter!" Molly turned to greet him. Setting her hands on his shoulders, she raised herself on her tiptoes and planted a kiss on his jaw. "You're here and that's what counts!"

They all walked up the driveway and were almost at the front door when the boys came running out. Yelling "Hi, Uncle Matt!" they threw themselves upon him and with a chuckle, he swung them both up in turn.

"Hey, guys, what have you been up to?"

"I beat my teacher at chess today," Iain announced as he hung onto Matt's arm. "And got a free hot dog!"

"Good for you," Matt said. "Way to go, kiddo!"

"And Frannie won a baseball bat in the hospital lottery!" Stuart danced backward along the path in front of them. "And she gave it to me! Cool, right?"

"*Très* cool!" Matt paused as they reached the trellised archway at the door. "Boys, you haven't met Ms. Rossiter—"

Liz broke in. "Matt, they don't need to be so formal. Liz is fine."

So Liz it was. And after a few moments' initial shyness, the boys accepted her happily in their midst. Once inside they insisted she see their rooms and with a laugh, she allowed herself to be led off, while Molly and Matt headed for the kitchen.

The boys' rooms were bright and airy, with posters on the walls, and trophies and toys and games lying on every surface. Iain had a hamster called Roly in a cage by the closet; Stuart had a sleek gray cat called Slim curled up like a snake on his bed. The window was wide-open and Liz could see a small backyard crammed with pretty flowers.

"Boys!" Molly's voice drifted through. "Wash your hands, we're going to eat now!"

The boys scurried into the bathroom together, and Liz wandered through to the kitchen. She found Matt leaning against the sink, a beer can in his hand, while Molly was taking a delicious-smelling lasagna out of the oven.

Matt didn't notice her. He was staring at his beer can and seemed lost in his thoughts...and those thoughts had provoked him into a black scowl.

She cleared her throat and he raised his head sharply. Then she saw him deliberately raise his eyebrows to wipe away the scowl.

"Oh, hi," he said pleasantly, and put down his can. "What'll you have to drink?"

"Oh...I guess a glass of pop?"

"I have some chilled cranberry juice." Molly blew back a wisp of hair and put the lasagna dish on a cork mat on the counter. "Or iced tea?" She pulled back a chair at the long kitchen table. "Sit here, Liz."

"Cranberry juice would be great. Thanks, Molly."

"Matt, would you pour a couple of glasses?" Molly took four plates from the warming drawer. "I'll have some, too."

It was obvious by the way Matt moved around the kitchen that this was like a second home to him.

It was also obvious to Liz that something was bothering him.

But what could it be?

She didn't think he was still angry with her. And she didn't think he resented her being there. In fact, after he set her glass of cranberry juice on the table, he placed a hand lightly on her shoulder, let it linger for a moment, his fingertips warm at her nape, before moving away again.

The gesture had been reassuring. Comforting.

But...why had he made it?

What was going on?

Matt wished he could spill out his problem to Liz. But she was the last person he could tell. At least, just now. Once he had everything sorted out, then he could explain.

Hoping no one had noticed his distracted mood, he tried to concentrate his attention on his food and on the conversation going on around him; but it was difficult, because all he could think of was the conversation he'd accidentally overheard earlier in the day.

He'd arranged to meet a client for lunch, but at the last minute the client had called to cancel, so he'd decided to work through the lunch hour. He'd got up to hunt for a file in the cabinet by his door, and at first when he heard Frannie chatting on the phone, he paid no attention. Not until he heard his own name did his ears prick up.

"...and the kids are crazy about Matt, too. Anyway, there'll be a wedding soon, Molly's *sooooo* excited, but don't tell a *soul* because Matt hasn't popped the question yet, but according to Molly, he's working himself up to it and any day now..."

Jaw hanging open, Matt had stood frozen. And wondering if he'd taken leave of his senses.

"...so that's all the news that's fit to print," Frannie said with a chuckle. "And anyway I have a dentist's appointment in five minutes so I have to dash. Talk to you tomorrow."

Seconds later, he heard Frannie leave her desk, open then shut the door to the street.

And silence reigned in the office again.

Except for the frantic thudding of his heart and the blood pounding in his ears.

Molly thought he was going to *propose* to her? Where on earth had she got that idea? And how many people had she told? Frannie believed it, Liz believed it...for all he knew, everyone in town believed it.

He suppressed a groan. Now, when he told Molly she'd been laboring under a delusion—as he had planned to do this evening before Liz had been invited along, too—she would think, mistakenly, that he was dumping her because Liz had come back into his life, whereas nothing could be further from the truth.

"Matt?" Molly's voice was concerned. "That was a mighty heavy sigh. Is something wrong?"

He blinked, and saw they were all looking at him.

Somehow he managed a rueful laugh. "Just thinking about work. Sorry, folks, I'll try to do better!"

And he did. He joined in the conversation, and after dinner when they all went to the park, he played ball with the boys, before taking Liz and Molly for a walk up the riverside path—the walk he'd promised Liz that morning.

They returned to the house around nine, and as soon as they got inside, the boys dragged him down to the basement to see a project they'd been working on. After a few minutes, he went upstairs again, while they stayed behind.

He found Molly in the kitchen.

"Where's Liz?" he asked.

"In the bathroom." She chuckled. "I well remember those frequent trips during pregnancy. One of the joys…"

"And another of the joys, apparently, is feeling tired in the evening. I'm going to take Liz home now."

"You're going so soon?" Molly didn't hide her disappointment.

And when he saw her crestfallen expression, he realized it was imperative that he set the record straight without delay, before any more damage was done.

"Yeah. But…I want to talk to you. Privately. Can I come back…once you've put the boys down for the night?"

She brightened up immediately. "Of course. I'll be putting them to bed in about half an hour. I'll expect you when?"

"Around ten."

Eyes sparkling she murmured, "We can sit out on the porch swing, it's a beautiful evening. A full moon, too!" She touched his cheek and looked up at him tenderly. "I'll look forward to it, honey."

Liz chose that moment to come back into the kitchen. She stood in the doorway, her eyes dark, her face pale.

Matt felt an awkward tension in the air, and to break it he said, "You look beat, Liz. I'm going to take you home."

She grimaced. "I'm sorry to be such a party pooper, but yes, I would like to go now, if you don't mind."

On the way back to Laurel House, she was quiet. And Matt, worriedly trying to figure out the least hurtful way to tell Molly she'd misread his intentions, made no effort to draw her out of her silence.

But once they got home, before Liz went upstairs, she apologized again for breaking up the evening.

"I truly am sorry, Matt. I know Molly expected us to stay longer, and she did go to so much trouble, and put on a lovely dinner."

"It's okay. I'm going back over there."

"Then I'll see you in the morning. Good night, Matt."

"Good night," he said softly.

But as he turned away, his thoughts had already turned back to Molly, as he wondered how she was going to react when he told her that he saw her only as a friend.

CHAPTER NINE

LIZ found Matt already in the kitchen when she went downstairs the next morning.

She greeted him with a cheery "Hi." And then because the kitchen door was wide-open, she walked over and looked out. The sky was china-blue and cloudless, and the white roses clambering up the pink brick wall gave off a heavenly fragrance.

"It's going to be another lovely day," she said as she turned back into the room.

Matt was putting a pot of tea on the table, along with a rack of whole wheat toast. "Yeah."

He'd already been for his run and the burnished copper highlights shone in his sable-black hair, which still glistened from his shower. He looked dynamic and flagrantly male in a black T-shirt and taupe chinos but she saw that his eyes were strained, his features tightly drawn.

"Sit down," he said. "Would you like a boiled egg? Or maybe a—"

"No, thanks. Just tea and toast will be fine. I'm not very hungry. I think I had too much of Molly's delicious lasagna last night." She took her seat and as she made a play of arranging the folds of the khaki cotton shirt she was wearing over her new white capri pants, she said, in a deliberately offhand tone, "I didn't hear you come in last night. Were you late?"

"No."

His tersely spoken response made it obvious he
didn't want to discuss it so Liz changed the subject.

"You're not forgetting my doctor's appointment at
ten-thirty?"

"No."

"Are you planning to go in to the office for a while
and then come back for me?"

"No. I have things to do here."

Conversation over breakfast was sparse. His mood
was as dour as it had been on the way to Molly's the
night before, so she let him stew in it. After they'd
eaten, and arranged their dishes in the dishwasher, he
excused himself.

"I'm going to be working out back. If I'm not in
by ten, give me a shout."

And with that, he took off.

Liz had never known Matt to be moody, and as she
went upstairs, she wondered what on earth was going
on between him and Molly.

She was in the bathroom brushing her teeth when
she heard a series of thudding sounds coming from the
backyard below.

Peeking out the window, she saw Matt over by the
garden shed. He was chopping wood, wielding the ax
like a madman; attacking the hefty blocks as if they
were a mortal enemy.

Mesmerized, Liz stared at him. Whatever emotion
was hounding him, it seemed likely he was using this
violent exercise in an effort to work it out.

She watched him for a few minutes longer and then,
with a sigh, she moved away from the window. She
hated to see Matt upset, but whatever his problem was,
it had nothing to do with her; so although he continued
to crash the ax into the wood with ferocious regularity

right up until ten o'clock, she didn't look out at him again.

"Everything's fine," Dr. Black said after he'd examined Liz. "And you're feeling better? You've had a total rest?"

"Yes, and Matt's treating me as if I were an invalid! He hasn't even let me do any driving," she added with a laugh, "the past couple of weeks."

"Well, if you get the chance to be a lady of leisure, I advise you to take it. But you're okay to drive yourself around—as long as you don't take another cross-country trip. That last one didn't do you any good."

"I know." Liz got up from her chair. "But I didn't want to leave my car behind. It was bequeathed to me by a dear friend of my mother's—it was the only time in her life that Melissa had ever splurged on anything but she bought it when she retired and she absolutely *adored* her little Porsche...and we had many happy trips in it so it meant a lot to me, too—though I admit now that in driving all the way from New York I bit off more than I could chew."

"I'll say!" The doctor walked her to the waiting room, and glanced around. "Matt's not here with you?"

"He parked across the street at his office. I'm to meet him there and he's going to drive me home."

"Make an appointment to see me again in two weeks. In the meantime, take care."

When Liz went out to the street a couple of minutes later, after the air-conditioned clinic the heat hit her like the blast from a 500 degree oven. The sun was blistering hot, and by the time she'd crossed the road, she could feel perspiration gathering on her brow.

But as she stepped onto the sidewalk, her attention was caught by an arrangement of plants outside a nearby florist's. So instead of going directly to Matt's office, she headed for the colorful display.

After browsing for a while, she selected a pink-blossomed hibiscus plant set in a heavy ceramic pot.

As she paid for it, she said to the clerk, ''Can you keep it for me? I'll have someone drop by and pick it up.''

Leaving the florist's, she made her way into Matt's office building, and smiled at the receptionist, who'd glanced up as she heard the door open.

''Hi,'' Liz said cheerfully. ''Is Matt in his office?''

The woman snapped, ''Yes, go in.'' And turning her back abruptly, busied herself with some files.

Well, wasn't *she* in a mood about something! Making a small face at the woman's back, Liz crossed to Matt's door. After a quick rat-tat, she walked in.

But here, the atmosphere was just as tense. When Matt looked up from his desk, his features were set in a scowl.

''Oh,'' he said, ''it's you.'' And though he at least attempted a smile, it didn't reach his eyes. He got up and came around the desk.

''So,'' he said, ''how did it go? Everything okay?''

''Yes, everything's fine.'' Was it *her* fault that he, like Frannie, was in a bad mood? She could see how it might irritate them both, that she was breaking into their busy schedule. ''Matt, I'm sorry to have taken up your time this morning, with the driving, I know how busy you are, the last thing you need is to see me coming into your office and—''

''Liz, believe me, seeing you is the *only* good thing that has happened today.'' He grasped her forearm and steered her unceremoniously to the door. "Let's get out of here."

Liz hurried to keep up with his long stride. What on earth was going on?

As they crossed the foyer, Matt said, "Frannie, I'll be out till after lunch. Page me if you need me."

The woman glanced up from her files, and Liz was astonished to see her throw her boss an even icier look than the one she'd given Liz.

"Will do." Frannie's tone was frigid, her head already bent again over her files.

Liz heard Matt swear under his breath.

And she felt him grip her arm even more tightly as he propelled her out to the street, and along the sidewalk toward his car.

Passing the florist's, she was reminded of her purchase and indicating the store, she said, "By the way, Matt, I bought a plant in there, for your mother, a small gesture of appreciation for her kindness. Could you pick it up when it's convenient and deliver it for me?"

"Naomi's gone away for the weekend," he said in a distracted tone, "but sure, I'll drop it off. In fact—" he changed direction and guided her toward the store's entrance "—we may as well do it now."

They collected the plant, which Matt set on the floor in the back of the car, carefully so as not to disturb the blossoms.

Then he drove along Main Street, and down Fifth Avenue, a narrow road that ran along the river to the east end of town. When he made a left onto a cul-de-sac lined with cherry trees, Liz said, "Your mother still lives in the same house, after all these years."

"Yeah, but it was rented then. Now it's hers." Matt

kept his eyes front as he swept the Taurus onto a single driveway and pulled the vehicle to a halt. "Her landlord moved out of town five years ago, gave Naomi the option to buy it. She'd always liked the place, so she jumped at the chance.'

"You liked it, too, I remember." Liz's gaze took in the modest yellow rancher, with its white picket fence and its tidy garden bright with nasturtiums and petunias and orange poppies. "You always said that although you and your mom never had much money, she knew how to make a house a home."

"Yeah, she did.''

Matt still seemed distracted. And Liz looked at him vexedly. "Matt, I hate to see you so uptight, I really *am* sorry to be eating into your time this way."

He turned in his seat. "Liz, you're *not* eating into my time. I didn't plan on going back to the office this morning, after you were finished in the clinic. I was going to drive you home, and I intended to stay and have lunch with you. There's something I have to tell you."

"What's happened, Matt? I couldn't help noticing that your receptionist was very...unfriendly...to me just now."

He didn't swear again, but she sensed that he wanted to. "Not only to you, but to me, too." His eyes were hard. "It's a mess, Liz. A bloody mess." He shook his head irritably. "Let's get this plant into the house, then we'll go out back and have our talk there."

Containing her impatience to hear his story, Liz followed him up the steps to the door and into the house.

Matt went first, carrying the plant, and Liz followed him into a small, attractively furnished sitting room.

There was a perfect spot for the hibiscus by the bay window.

After Matt had set it down, he stood back.

"There," he said. "Will that do?"

"Yes, that's great. Thanks, Matt."

Liz glanced around. On the coffee table were piles of *Good Housekeeping* magazines, a couple of mystery paperbacks and a bowl of potpourri that gave off a powdery perfume.

"Naomi won't mind your bringing me here," she asked, "while she's not at home?"

"Of course not. When I tell her we were here, she'll wish she could have been at home so she could have made you a cup of tea. Can I make you one now?"

"No, I'm fine." Liz's gaze moved to a glass-doored bookcase to one side of the hearth. But instead of holding books, it was crammed with trophies.

Boxing trophies.

She moved over and crouched down in front of them. "I had no idea that you had so many."

"It's all in the past." His tone was dismissive.

"Yes, but still…" Her gaze flicked from trophy to trophy to trophy—

"Liz." He spoke curtly. "Let's go outside."

He'd given up boxing because he'd been badly beaten; she knew that. But she still didn't know how it had happened, or who the woman was he had fought over.

There was no point in asking him. He wouldn't tell her.

But one day, she might ask Naomi.

In the meantime, she pushed it to the back of her mind, and went with Matt through a galley-style kitchen and out to a private backyard with a six-foot high fence, three apple trees, hanging baskets dangling from hooks under the low eaves…and, to Liz's great surprise, a swimming pool with sparkling blue waters and a blue-and-white tiled apron.

"Matt, I didn't know you had a pool! I was never in this house before, of course, but I don't recall your ever saying—"

"We didn't have a pool here when I was growing up. My mother's landlord put it in, six years ago. He'd planned on moving into this house when he retired and his wife loved to swim. But she died before they could make the move, and he decided to relocate to Vancouver Island. Naomi really didn't want a pool…it's a lot of work, but I take care of it for her. And actually use it more than she does!"

"It looks tempting right now!" Liz said idly, and tugged her shirt away from her back as she felt it sticky with perspiration. "This is the hottest day we've had so far."

"You fancy a dip?"

She turned startled eyes to Matt. "Oh, no, I—"

"Naomi keeps an extra couple of swimsuits for when friends drop by."

"No, Matt, I don't think—"

"Oh, come on. It'll do us both good to cool off."

"I thought you wanted to talk to me."

"I do. But it can wait."

She looked at his strained face, his tired eyes. And she wanted to smooth the frown lines on his brow; wanted to kiss his worries away. Instead she told herself to smarten up, because inviting him to intimacy was the very last thing she should be doing. She did want to see his tension eased, though, and if a swim would help, then…

"Okay," she said, "if you can find a swimsuit for me."

He was away for about four minutes and when he came back, he was wearing only a pair of black swim trunks. Uh-oh, Liz thought; this was a huge mistake. She would just have to make sure she kept to the opposite end of the pool from him once she got in the water.

He held out a handful of primrose-yellow fabric.

"Here," he said. "This should keep you decent."

Decent, Liz mused wryly as she saw her reflection in Naomi's bathroom mirror, was not the word she would have used to describe how she looked in the miniscule bikini. Her small breasts had swollen with pregnancy and her hips were more rounded, so her figure, which she normally thought of as "trim," now seemed positively voluptuous!

And she wasn't about to let Matt feast his eyes on it. The last thing she wanted was to titillate him. So she grabbed up a towel and wrapped it around herself before she went back outside.

But Matt was already in the water and swimming away from her, so she was able to throw off the towel and get into the pool without being noticed.

She started swimming lengths, and it was glorious. The water felt like silk. Lucky Matt, that he could come here anytime he liked. Once she regained possession of Laurel House, she would have to think about having a pool put in.

She swam and dreamed and counted lengths.

And as she finished her tenth, at the deep end, she grasped the lip of the pool and took a breather.

Matt surged to the surface right beside her and

planted a big hand on the tiled apron, just inches from her own.

He grinned at her—a flash of white teeth, a dazzle of green eyes—and she felt herself grow weak with the wraparound intimacy of his smile. Of him. Of his closeness.

And she realized with a feeling of dismay that instead of worrying in case her new voluptuous figure might arouse Matt, she should have been worrying about the effect he had on her!

"So," he drawled, "how was it?"

His hair was plastered to his brow and beads of water streamed down his ridged nose and around his mouth and down over his chin. She wanted to reach out and follow their path with her fingertip; she wanted to sway toward him in the luxuriously sensuous water and slide against his body.

"It was lovely." Her voice came out breathlessly and she hoped he'd put it down to the exertion of her swim. "Blissful, actually."

"Blissful it is," he murmured. "Odd," he went on amusedly, "I've been using this pool for years and it's never been this...blissful...before."

He was flirting with her. It seemed harmless, yet Liz felt a sexual tension between them that was anything but harmless. They were alone here, and half naked, and the physical attraction between them had always been undeniable. The situation was potentially explosive. She decided to defuse it by pretending to take his comment at face value.

"Maybe you've never been so stressed-out before," she said lightly. "And then it's so very hot today, you're appreciating the water more than usual."

"Yeah. That could be it. Or—" the intensity of his

gaze arrowed right into her soul, making it want to dive for cover "—it could be that swimming with the most beautiful woman in the world is what makes it so blissful."

"Ah, how fickle is the male of the species!"

"How so?"

"Didn't you tell me that you had once lost a fight over the most beautiful woman in the world and instead of winning the woman you got this!" She tapped his broken nose flippantly. "And this!" She touched his flat cheek. "And this!" She ran the tip of her index finger over the thin scar on his lip...but before she could drop her hand he grabbed her wrist roughly...and held it.

Jolted, she shot her gaze to his eyes and saw that his expression was no longer amused, but hard.

"Fickle isn't something I care to be called, Liz."

"Then you ought to be more careful how you label your lovers! You can't have two who were both, to you, the most beautiful women in the world!" Haughtily she glared back at him. "Now *can* you!"

"No, Liz," he returned steadily. "I can't. And what's more," he added, "I didn't. You are...and always have been, to me...the most beautiful woman in the world. That other woman, the one I loved and lost so many years ago, was you."

"Matt, I—"

"I don't want to get into this right now." Matt swore silently. Sheer pride. That's what had made him say as much as he had. Which was already too much. But hearing Liz call him "fickle" had been too much for him to take. He had never been unfaithful to her.

She snatched her wrist free from his grip. "You can't say something like that and just leave it!" she said. "You haven't even told me who you were fighting with!"

"It's in the past, Liz. It's the present that matters. And that's what I need to talk to you about." He grabbed the lip of the pool and bracing himself, surged up out of the water and stood on the tiled apron. Bending over toward her, he held out a hand. "Come on out..."

But she spurned his help. And diving away from him she made for the far end of the pool, with long elegant strokes. Climbing up the ladder, she crossed to the patio and scooped up her towel. Tipping her head to one side, she started to dry her hair.

He walked around the pool toward her. Decent? He'd thought the yellow bikini would keep her *decent?* Huh! She would probably have looked more decent naked, because the yellow scraps of fabric made what was hidden seem all the more tantalizingly erotic. Hidden fruits, forbidden fruits. He felt himself becoming aroused and decided he'd better make a speedy retreat.

He headed past her, making for the patio doors. "I'll be back in a minute," he said over his shoulder. "Fancy something to drink?"

"Maybe a glass of iced water?"

He stayed inside till he had himself under control.

When he went out again, the white towel was lying crumpled on a chaise and Liz was tucking a cosmetic bag into her purse. Her hair was smooth, two brush strokes of wheat-gold, curving downward from her middle parting, over her tanned shoulders and ending in two fans over her breasts.

She looked delicate as a fairy, yet her eyes, as they fixed on him, were too wordly-wise to be a fairy's eyes. And they watched him warily as he approached with her water.

"Thanks," she said. And took several sips from the glass before setting it down on the patio table.

"Let's sit over here." He led her to a bench under one of the apple trees. "It'll be cooler, in the shade."

Brushing a few dead leaves from the white-painted wood, he indicated that she should sit down. She did. He did not. For what he was about to say, he preferred to remain standing.

She looked up at him, questioningly. And waited.

He'd always liked that about her, that she could live with silence, that she sensed when to speak, when not to.

"Now that I finally have you here," he said, with a self-derisive laugh, "I haven't a clue where to start."

"Then why not start at the end!" she returned, teasing him. "And work your way back."

"That might not be a bad idea. Okay." He inhaled a deep breath. "Molly doesn't want to see me again."

Liz's eyes clouded, but other than that, her expression gave nothing away. "I don't need to ask how that has made you feel," she said quietly. "I've seen how upset you've been, since your visit last night. Is there any chance you can patch things up with her?" Liz frowned suddenly. "But why doesn't she want to see you again? I thought…it certainly seemed to me…that Molly was crazy about you!"

"I guess," Matt said, "starting at the end isn't really going to work. Let me fill you in on the background."

He told Liz of the promise he'd made to Dave, and told her of his efforts to live up to that promise.

"What I didn't realize was that Molly had misread

my attentions. She somehow got the impression that I…was in love with her, and she'd said as much to several people. Word had got around that I was working up to propose. And when I discovered that, I knew I had to set the record straight, and that's why I went back to see her last night.''

"And you told her—''

"I told her I thought of her only as a friend. She was hysterical, I had a helluva job trying to calm her down…and then in the end she went frighteningly cold and quiet and told me she never wanted to see me again.''

Liz didn't say anything for a long moment, and then she said, "I'm really sorry you've had this misunderstanding with Molly, Matt. But…it's a private affair, between the two of you. Why…are you telling me about it?''

"Because you're involved.''

"Me? But…how?''

"Molly thinks that everything would have gone on the way she expected it to go on—love and marriage and happy-ever-after—if you hadn't come back to town. She believes, you see, that I've dumped her for someone else. And she believes that that someone else is you.''

He could see the dismay in Liz's eyes. She lurched to her feet. "But it's not true, Matt. I've never done anything to come between the two of you. I've told you already that I no longer even find you attractive! Can't you tell her that? At least, if she knew there was nothing between us, knew that for sure, she might begin to accept that she had misread all your kindness to her and the boys?''

"I can't say it, Liz.''

"But why not?" she demanded fiercely. "Why not, if it's true?"

He shook his head. "But it's not true, is it?" he said softly. "It'll never be over, between you and me."

Tears welled up in her eyes, quenching the fire. "Matt, how many times do I have to tell you—"

"What *you* tell me, and what your *eyes* tell me, are two different things."

She turned away from him but not before he'd seen a tear spill over and trickle down her cheek.

With a groan, he caught her and whirled her around to face him. Then with his hands on her shoulders, he pulled her to him. "Liz," he whispered. "Oh, Liz…"

He kissed her then…and she didn't even try to resist. She melted against him, and kissed him back with a passion that made his knees tremble. On and on they kissed, his fingers tangled in her hair, his head filled with the smell of chlorine, his heart filled with the joy of having her in his arms.

When she finally drew back, breathlessly, her cheeks were flushed, her lips swollen.

"Tell me now," he said thickly, "that you no longer want me."

She stepped back, and came up against the trunk of the apple tree. "You know I can't." Her voice quavered. "But I don't always take what I want."

"Even when it's freely offered?"

Numbly she shook her head. "I told you, Matt. I'm on my own, and that's the way I like it. You'd be wise not to waste any more time thinking things will ever be the same between us as they once were. It'll never happen."

He could see, by the steely glint in her eyes, that

he didn't have a hope of changing her mind. Not at this moment. But today he had made a major step in the right direction: he'd kissed her and she had kissed him right back, and she had admitted that she still wanted him.

A few moments ago he'd admired the "waiting" quality she possessed. It was a quality he had, too. In spades.

And he was not going to give up till she finally took what she wanted. No matter how long that took.

She was right on one point: things could never be the same between them again. They would be different. And it was his hope and his prayer that they could be even better. They were both older, they both knew that love wasn't enough; two people had to work at a relationship. And he intended to give it everything he had in his power to give.

But he would take it slowly. One day at a time.

"I'm sorry," he said, "if I've upset you. But," he added as she would have spoken, "I'm not sorry I kissed you. There are some things—" he threw her a boyish grin to defuse the tension between them "—that a red-blooded guy has just gotta do when he sees a cute gal in a bikini! Now—" he grabbed her hand, and swinging it, led her up the lawn towards the house "—let's go home. I'm starving!"

As they drove back out to the street a few minutes later, Liz said, "Matt, the night you took Molly to the barn dance, I heard you come in after four and I thought..."

"You thought—oh, you thought *that!* Uh-uh. Iain was sick, he wanted me to stay. Which I did." He sent her a teasing glance. "So...any other wicked thoughts?"

She wrinkled her nose. "Just...I saw a wispy lacy bra in your laundry one day, and I thought—"

"What a very busy—and naughty!—little mind you have, Miss Rossiter." He chuckled. "It would have been Naomi's. My mother often takes her washing to the house and runs it through with mine. That's it? Anything more?"

She shook her head. And then looked at him worriedly. "Matt, what are you going to do about Molly? Are you going to try to talk to her?"

He sobered. "She's hurt and humiliated and angry. She's not ready to listen to anything I have to say."

"But...what about the boys? Won't they miss you?"

"The school term ends next week. Molly always takes them down to her parents in Vancouver for the first month of the summer holidays. Maybe by the time she gets back, she won't feel so...hostile toward me...and we can mend our bridges then."

Molly did leave for Vancouver the following week, and she didn't contact Matt or Liz before she left.

Naomi heard about it all on the grapevine and though she was sympathetic toward Molly, she assured Liz that Matt had never treated Molly as anything other than a friend.

"She needed someone to depend on after Dave died, and Matt filled that need. It's time she stood on her own two feet, what she needs is to start working again. And what *you* need to do, Liz, is to stop concerning yourself about Molly and focus on getting ready for your darling baby!"

CHAPTER TEN

Liz took Naomi's advice and she found that the following weeks passed quickly.

She kept well; saw Dr. Black regularly; rested every afternoon; and walked after dinner every evening with Matt.

She looked forward to those walks, which had soon become the highlight of her day.

They avoided talking about Laurel House and their upcoming battle over it. The only thing they ever argued about—and they argued about it just once—was Liz's refusal to attend Lamaze classes.

Matt had brought the subject up one evening when they were strolling along a sun-dappled path that meandered through the woods behind the house.

"Moms-to-be are supposed to take those classes," he said. "With a partner."

"I don't have a partner."

He quirked an eyebrow. "I don't suppose you'd consider—"

"No! I would *not* care to lie flat on my back with my belly in the air and you sitting cross-legged beside me, whispering sweet nothings in my ear in time to soothing music!" But despite her indignant rejection of his offer, she couldn't help smiling at the image it conjured up.

"You could go on your own, then. Just be part of the group. I'm sure there are other women who go on their own."

She watched a crimson-and-white butterfly flit up from a wildflower and disappear amid the leafy branches of an alder tree. "I'm not other women, Matt, and I don't like to join things! I like to be independent."

"But you'd learn how to relax."

"I *know* how to relax. I read a book on relaxation last time around and mastered the technique, and I practice it faithfully every afternoon when I lie down for my nap."

"But you'd also learn how to breathe properly—"

"I know how to breathe properly!"

"—and how to pant and when to push—"

"How to *pant? When* to *push?*" She gaped at him incredulously. "Matt, did you keep that book—"

"Well, yeah. I did. Actually I find it very—"

"I don't believe this! I told you—"

"I know. But, Liz, I want to help." Intensity had darkened his eyes to a deep hunter-green. "You may not need my help, but I need to give it."

"Yes," she said with a quiet sigh. "I know."

"And I think you know why."

"Yes, I know why." He wanted to redeem himself for having let her down when she'd told him she was expecting his baby. He couldn't. She knew he was sorry, but sorry wasn't enough. The scales were too unevenly balanced and nothing he could do now would *ever* tip his side up so it was raised to the level of what she'd suffered alone.

"Then please don't shut me out."

They'd stopped walking, and a beam of sunshine slanted between two trees and gleamed like topaz on his hair. He was so close that over the forest smells of moss and resin, she could smell his unique male scent, as familiar to her now as it had been thirteen years ago. It still drew her in ways she didn't understand. And it made her yearn to press her lips to his throat, and inhale that erotic scent—

"Liz?"

She was tempted…oh, so tempted…to give in. To let him help. It would feel so good to spill out her worries, to confess how afraid she was that something would go wrong with this pregnancy. But if she did, she would forfeit more than she would gain; she would forfeit her independence.

"It's important to me," she said, "to take charge of my own life."

"I don't want to take charge of your life. I just want to help."

"The best way you can help is to let me do things in my own way."

He let the matter drop.

And he didn't ever mention the Lamaze classes again.

But he continued to study his baby book.

He didn't bother hiding it from her now. She would come on it where she least expected it. One time, it was in the laundry room; another time on the kitchen windowsill; once she even found it in the garage. But more often than not, it was on the coffee table in the sitting room. It had a well-thumbed look, and each time she saw it, he'd moved his page marker onto a different chapter.

Curiosity had made her peek; and she noticed he was keeping pace with her pregnancy. She noticed, also, that he had used a yellow highlighter to mark certain passages.

One Saturday afternoon when she came down from

her nap, she found the book, lying open, on the kitchen table. She glanced at it, and saw he was reading the chapter entitled: Preparing The Baby's Nursery.

She poured herself a glass of milk and sitting at the table, pulled the book over. But before she could start reading, Matt came in from outside.

"Oh, hi," he said. "I see you're having a squint at my book. Good. I want to discuss something with you."

"What?"

"I know you want a yellow-and-white nursery and—"

"How on earth do you know that?"

"I overheard you telling the clerk when I lined up behind you to buy the mobile that night. So...what I want to know is, do you want the walls painted yellow...or were you thinking the walls should be white and perhaps the blinds yellow, or maybe the carpet—"

"Why do you want to know?"

"I've decided to turn that second guest room—the one Naomi was working on—into a nursery for the new baby."

Liz narrowed her gaze. "Does that mean you're planning to give up on fighting me for the house?"

"Heck no! But either way—whether the house is yours or mine—you'll be coming back here from the hospital, at least for a while, and you'll need a room for the baby. I figure that since the guest room adjoins your bedroom, it'll make an ideal nursery. So...that takes me back to my question. White walls or yellow? I've arranged with Naomi to do the painting at her own convenience."

Liz hesitated, and then said, "I was planning to have the walls primrose yellow and the trim a nice glossy white. And I thought...perhaps a Disney border for the walls.''

"How about buying that crib, the one with the mobile over it? It had Disney decals and would go nicely with your scheme. I could drive over to Crestville tomorrow and pick it up for you.''

"Heavens, I'm not planning to buy the very first crib I see! Half the fun of buying for a baby is browsing. And when I go shopping for the crib, I'll be looking at sheets, too, and blankets, and...all *sorts* of things.''

"Can I ask you something personal?''

"Sure. But whether I answer will depend on whether I mind the question!''

"How are you off for money? I mean, you haven't been working now for months. And your father didn't leave you a bean.''

"I earned good money in New York, and I've saved a fair bit. I can afford to splurge on this baby. I'm looking forward to going back to the Sagebrush Mall. I'll make an outing of it.''

"We'll make an outing of it together.''

"Matt, men like shopping at places like Canadian Tire where they can gaze for hours at a box of nails! Baby Departments do *not* turn them on! If you were with me, you'd be hovering in the background and I'd feel rushed.''

"I'll go to the bookstore. Look,'' he went on quickly as she made to argue, "if you're planning a major shopping spree, you'll need me to carry everything. And you did say, last time, that you appreciated having me as a chauffeur. Now.'' He glanced pointedly at the rounded bulge under her crisp shirt. "I should think you'd appreciate it even more.''

"You," she said, "are *s-o-o-o* pushy."

"Yeah." He grinned. "That I am."

She thought of trailing around the department store for hours, her back probably aching even worse than it was regularly doing now, carting everything out to her car, then facing the long drive home. She nibbled her lip.

And he saw her uncertainty. "It would be better," he said coaxingly, "for the baby, if I did the driving."

"I have to say one thing, you sure know the right buttons to press! Okay, I'll let you do the driving. And thanks for the offer. What time shall we leave?"

Liz took an early nap the next day and they left for Crestville at two o'clock.

When they arrived at the mall, they went directly to the Baby Department at the Bay.

Matt said, "Let's see if that crib is still here."

It was. And Matt seemed to have set his heart on it, Liz mused. But as he inspected it, she moved on to look at the others on display. There were seven in all.

She decided the first one had been the nicest.

And she told Matt so when she walked back to him.

"So you'll take it? I talked to a salesperson and she said you can buy matching Disney borders at the paint shop at the other end of the mall. I'll go get them while you carry on with your shopping."

"Where will we meet up?"

"I'll come back here. What time?"

"Give me till five o'clock."

He took off whistling, apparently enjoying himself as much as she was.

After asking a salesperson to set aside one of the boxed cribs and a mattress, Liz shopped eagerly. She ended up buying a couple of sets of yellow-and-white bed linens and a package of diapers and six patterned receiving blankets and four tiny undershirts and the sweetest yellow-and-white knit romper suit that she'd ever seen.

Time passed so quickly that when five came around, she noticed the time with a sense of shock. She paid for all her purchases, and had just turned from the Service desk, laden with packages, when she saw Matt approach.

''You look,'' he said, ''as if you've bought up the store!''

She laughed. ''I warned you.''

''Where's the crib?''

''We have to pick it up at the side entrance.''

He took all the packages from her save a couple of the lighter ones. ''So,'' he said as they walked along the mall, ''how are you feeling?''

''Wilting, I'm afraid.''

''Glad I came along?'' he teased.

''Yes,'' she said sincerely. ''I really am.''

''Tell you what,'' he said as they walked outside, ''let's have a bite to eat at that White Spot across the way, then when we get home, you can put your feet up and relax.''

They arrived home at seven-thirty.

As they walked in from the car, Matt glanced down at Liz. Her white shirt wasn't as crisp as it had been in the early afternoon, and her khaki skirt was creased, but she still looked absolutely gorgeous.

Her face was pale, though, and her eyes heavy.

''I hope,'' he said, ''that you haven't overdone it.''

''My back aches but then it usually does!''

He unlocked the door and they went into the foyer. The house felt hot and stuffy. He left the door open.

"Why don't you go out to the patio," he suggested. "It'll be pleasant in the shade. Put your feet up, I'll bring you a cold drink after I've carted all your purchases upstairs."

When he went outside a few minutes later, Liz was lying back on a chaise, a forearm over her eyes, her sandals under the table. Her long hair spilled over the arm of the chaise in a cascade of white-gold.

She was so still he thought she'd drifted off to sleep. But just then she made a *tsking* sound and shifted her right leg impatiently, as if it were uncomfortable.

He set the lemonade glass on the table. "Are you okay?"

She took her arm away and when she looked up at him, her smile was so endearingly sweet he felt his love for her well up inside him till he almost choked on it.

"It's so peaceful here," she said. "I'm almost ashamed to feel so lazy." She crinkled her nose. "The only thing that's spoiling it is my right leg's been cramping a bit."

He loved the way she crinkled her nose; it made him want to kiss it. Instead he crouched down alongside the chaise. "Here, let me."

He wrapped her slender foot in his hands, massaged it gently. She didn't resist or try to pull away.

"Stretch out your leg," he murmured. She did. He held her toes and pressed the heel down. "Tell me," he said, "when you feel the stretch in your calf muscle."

He worked on her for a few minutes, stretching the leg, massaging the foot, trying to concentrate on his task and not get distracted by the exquisite fineness of her bones or the seductive smoothness of her skin or the daintiness of her pink-painted toenails.

"Thanks, Matt," she said when he finally released her and stood up. "That felt wonderful." She ran her fingers through her hair, and then gathering it back in two handfuls, tucked the long glossy tassels behind her ears. "Could you pass me my lemonade?"

"I'm going inside to exchange it for milk. If you're prone to having these cramps, you should be drinking more milk...or taking calcium tablets. It says so—"

"In your baby book." She shook her head, her expression wry. "You just don't give up, do you?"

"No," he said. "And I'm not going to. Whether you want my help or not, I plan on giving it to you until you have this baby safely in your arms."

He went inside. And as he poured Liz a glass of milk, he realized he hadn't felt this happy in months. No, in years.

And yet, at the back of his mind, there was always a niggling unrest. Because of Molly. She hadn't come back from Vancouver, as she usually did, at the end of July. It was now almost September, the schools would be going in next week, and she still hadn't returned home. He felt so badly that things had turned out between them the way it had; how unfortunate it was that she'd misread his intentions.

"Matt?" Liz had come padding into the kitchen in her bare feet. "What's wrong?"

"I was just thinking," he said, "about—"

An abrupt knock on the back door interrupted him.

He said, "Who the heck can that be, on a Sunday night?"

Liz gave a "beats me!" shrug and watched as he walked to the door.

He opened it, and blinked in surprise.

"Molly!" Stunned, he stared at the brunette who was standing on the step, her hands thrust aggressively into the pockets of her beige slacks. "When did you get back?"

"This afternoon. Matt, I have something to say to you."

She looked over his shoulder and a muscle twitched in her cheek when she saw Liz.

"Oh," she said. "You're here, too. That's good." She walked past Matt into the kitchen and whirled around to face him. "Because what I have to say concerns Liz, too."

"Molly," Matt said sharply, "keep Liz out of this. I won't have you upsetting her, she's in no condition to be—"

"I'm not going to upset Liz." Molly's voice trembled. "I promise."

"If you do, I'll—"

"Matt, I don't want to upset either of you. Actually—" she took in a very deep breath "—I've come to apologize, to say I'm truly sorry for the way I acted."

As Matt watched in astonishment, he saw tears well up in her eyes.

"The things I said." Her brown curls bobbed as she shook her head. "I've been stupid...and *incredibly* self-centered. After Dave died, I...well, I just felt so lost, and needing someone to lean on, and you were there for me. But I clung to you more and more, instead of learning to stand on my own two feet. You've been the best friend any woman could have and I think

I went crazy for a while, imagining you were in love with me...and believing I was in love with you when what I felt was really affection and tremendous gratitude because you'd done so much for me and the boys.''

Molly turned to Liz.

"Liz, I've been so unfair to you. I don't know if Matt told you this, but I blamed you for taking him away from me. Whatever's between you, it has nothing to do with me."

Liz hastened to say, "Molly, there's been nothing—"

"As I said, Liz, it's not my business. I didn't come here to pry. I came to apologize, and to tell Matt that I'm going to do something I should have done a year ago. I'm going back to work. I had a lot of time to think when I was at my parents', and I've decided to move down to Vancouver, where Mom can help out with the boys. I've taken a job at Vancouver General, I start next week." She gave Matt a watery smile. "I'm actually looking forward to it!"

"Molly, that's wonderful!" he said. "Congratulations." About to embrace her, he hesitated, and then said teasingly, "Is it okay if I give you a hug?"

"Oh, you can still hug me!" Molly gave a shaky laugh. "I won't read anything into it, I promise!"

So they hugged, and then Liz and Molly hugged, and Liz brushed back a few tears, and Matt said how he was going to miss her and the boys.

"I'll visit you every time I'm in the city," he said. "And whenever you feel you and the kids need a break, pop up for a holiday. You'll always be welcome."

Molly left soon after. "I need to get home," she

said. "I have loads of packing to do and I want to get started. Will you drop by soon, Matt, and visit with the boys?"

He assured her he would.

He and Liz walked out to her car with her.

Before Molly drove off, she said quietly, "I'll have a talk with Frannie, Matt. Before tomorrow night, she—and everyone else in town—will know just what a foolish woman I've been!"

Matt said, "Molly, you don't have to—"

"Oh, but I do." Molly's eyes had a determined glint. "I have to set the record straight."

After she'd driven away, Matt said to Liz,

"Well, thank heavens that got all sorted out."

"You've been worrying about her all summer, haven't you?"

"I felt I'd let Dave down. I took on responsibility for his family and I screwed up—I caused Molly more grief."

"Don't blame yourself." Liz had come out in her bare feet and now she felt the gravel bite into her soles as she made her way back across the forecourt. "Molly was lonely, and vulnerable...it must have been easy—and comforting—for her to believe she was in love with you...and vice versa."

He chuckled. "She said she went crazy for a while and she must have been. How else could she have taken a fancy to this battered old face!"

"Oh, I don't know," Liz said lightly. "It has a certain charm. It's possible that—ouch!" she yelped as a sharp stone bit into the ball of her foot. "Hey, that hurt! I should have put on my sandals!"

"Yeah, you should. But since you didn't—" Matt swept her up in his arms.

"Let me down, I'm far too heavy!"

"Heavy?" He rolled his eyes. "Sheesh, you weigh less than a feather. So," he went on as he ambled toward the house, "you think this old face has a certain charm?" He sounded smug.

What she was thinking had nothing to do with charm. And everything to do with sex. She was thinking how virile he was, and how feminine he made her feel. And how close her lips were to his throat, where she could see a pulse throbbing. She could also see beads of sweat on his chin, and could sense how rough that dark-shadowed jaw would feel if she were to cup her palm over it.

"Most women do like men to *look* like men," she said with an airiness she was far from feeling.

"I'm not interested in what most women like." He walked through the open kitchen doorway, swinging her sideways so she didn't hit the doorjamb either side. "I'm only interested in what *you* like."

He came to a stop in the middle of the kitchen and looked down at her. She could see three flecks of silver in the iris of his left eye, four in the right. She counted them while he held her hard against his fast-thudding heart.

"You can let me down now," she whispered. "I—"

He kissed her.

Passionately. Possessively. Desperately.

She couldn't have fought him even if she'd wanted to. Which she didn't. She was his for the taking.

His lips were warm, mobile, seeking. Demanding. And as his kiss deepened, although he gradually let her slide to her bare feet, he still held her imprisoned in his arms. As if he thought she might try to escape.

Nothing was further from her mind.

Her mind, in fact, had ceased to function and she was running on heart alone. Excitement and need rushed through her with the violence of a tornado, a whirlwind that sucked away her caution and sent it careening into oblivion. She wound her arms urgently around his neck and kissed him back with a feverish intensity that aroused him to a point where he couldn't hide it. Nor did he try to.

A low moan came from between her parted lips…a moan that became a gasp as his tongue stole in and sought out its mate, seducing it into a dance of desire that sent spirals of sensation sizzling to her core.

Arching against him like a wanton, she tightened her arms convulsively around his neck, and at the same time reveled in his raw animal scent. It filled her nostrils and incited her to a heady recklessness that made her forget everything except this man and what was happening between them.

When he finally drew back, he was breathing hard, and his eyes were dark, his cheeks flushed.

"We can't do this," he whispered. And pressed a trembling kiss to her damp brow.

"Do what?" she asked dizzily.

"What we both want to do." He curved a hand around her neck, his fingertips slick at her nape. "Make love."

"But—"

"I didn't mean to go this far." His eyes made love to her, though his body didn't. "You have to be very careful. We don't want to do anything that might harm this baby."

Slowly, slowly, Liz felt her delirium begin to fade, and as it did, she came gradually to her senses. Matt was right. She had to be very careful. She *wanted* to be very careful.

And thank heavens for his powers of self-control, for if it had been left to her, she'd have let him take her, right there where they stood.

And now…she was embarrassed.

And also angry with herself for having let him discover just how much of a slave she was to her passion for him.

"Matt, it won't happen again. I'm appalled at the way I behaved just now…please put it down to hormones run amok because of my pregnancy. I'm not in the least interested in making love to you, and under normal circumstances—"

"Don't, Liz."

Taken aback by his pained tone, she gazed up at him. His eyes were serious. And fixed on her steadily.

"Don't what?"

"Don't dismiss what just happened. You can say you're not interested in me, or in making love to me, but if you believe it, then you're fooling yourself. As I've said before, sweetheart, what we had between us will never be over. And what I'm saying now is, I'm not going to make love to you…not now, not yet. But after your baby's born and you've had enough time to recover, I'll be knocking at your door again. You can count on it."

Count on it?

Count on *him?*

She hadn't been able to count on him in the past. Why on earth would she be foolish enough to count on him now!

CHAPTER ELEVEN

SEPTEMBER passed.

Molly and family moved to Vancouver—after a wonderful farewell party put on by Frannie—and Naomi spent more and more time at Laurel House, first of all painting the baby's room, and then just visiting with Liz.

Matt's mother absolutely refused to let Liz assume the heavier housekeeping duties, so Liz had to be content with taking over the dusting and the general tidying and the laundry...and the cooking.

To Liz's delight, Naomi had been highly impressed with her culinary skills.

"What a *fabulous* meal!" the older woman had enthused, the first time Liz had invited her for dinner. "I haven't had salmon en croute in years, and it wasn't *half* as good as yours. Where on *earth* did you learn to cook like that?"

"Melissa—my mother's friend—was a home economics teacher. I couldn't even boil an egg when I went to live with her. She was horrified, and set about remedying the situation."

"Naomi's right." Matt had sat back contentedly in his chair. "You could cook your way into any man's heart." He shot her a teasing smile. "You've certainly cooked your way into mine!"

"Don't think," Liz had retorted, "that you can weasel your way back into my good books with flattery. It'll take more than a few overblown compliments to make up for what you did yesterday!''

Naomi cocked her ears. ''What did you do, Matt?''

His lips twitched. ''After I had the nursery carpeted, it looked bare with only the crib so I brought home a changing table and a nursing chair with a yellow cushion and—''

''And the sweetest little teddy bear you've ever seen, Naomi!'' Liz glared at Matt, and tried to look ferocious. ''You just *have* to be one step ahead, don't you! You knew I was planning to buy those items, you saw me circling them in the Bay flier that came in the mail last week!''

''I have never,'' Naomi said amusedly, ''known two people who bicker as much as you do!''

''Hey,'' Matt protested with mock-innocence, ''it's not my fault. I think we all know who's the bossy one around here!''

Ignoring him, Liz put her elbows on the table and leaned confidingly toward Naomi. ''I shall be glad,'' she said, ''when he goes away on his trip. He's getting to be a real pain in the neck.''

''You'll miss me,'' Matt said confidently.

''Huh!'' she said. ''You wish!''

But she knew, of course, that she would miss him. He was going to be leaving in a couple of weeks on his annual trip with three buddies he'd kept in touch with since law school. Last year they'd gone whitewater rafting in Oregon; the year before they'd gone scuba diving in Belize; and this year they had planned a camping trip in the Yukon.

The day before he left, she walked into her bedroom and found him by the bed.

''What are you doing?'' she asked.

"I've just put a board under the mattress. It'll help your back, it says so—"

"It says so in your book!" She threw up her hands. "What am I going to do with you?"

"I guess," he drawled, "I'm just a faster reader than you. What chapter are you on?"

She laughed. Couldn't help it. He was just so darned charming!

And when he returned from his trip—striding into the kitchen one afternoon out of the blue—she felt a dizzying rush of love. And even though he looked like a police Wanted poster with his black hair shaggy and his jaw darkly bearded, she had no will to resist when he put his arms around her bulky body and gave her a prolonged hug.

Then he pulled back and looked at her, his eyes warm with affection. But when he noticed the brown patches on her skin, around her nose, he frowned.

"What's this?" He ran a fingertip over the patches.

"It's nothing. Just—"

"Oh, yeah." Understanding dawned in his eyes and she saw them twinkle. "Chapter Seven, page 192. 'Brown patches on face, will go after the birth'!"

"Don't tell me you took that book with you on your trip!"

"Didn't have to. I read an extra couple of chapters ahead before I left." His gaze dropped to her bulge. And he did a double take. "Hey," he said, pretending shock, "you're beginning to look like a circus tent!"

She protested indignantly...but when he took a small cobaltblue box from his pocket—a jeweler's box—and held it out to her, her protests trailed away.

"What's this?" she asked.

"Open it."

It was a pendant—a dime-size crystal case suspended on a fine gold chain. Inside glimmered a mass of tiny flakes of gold.

Liz felt her eyes mist as she looked at it.

"We did some panning," he said casually. "What I found, I had made up for you. Like it?"

"Oh, Matt, it's *lovely*. And you really found this gold?"

"Yeah. Let me put it on for you."

Obediently she turned, and stood with her head down, scooping back her hair to give him access to her nape. He slipped the chain around her neck, and then concentrated on the delicate fastener. She felt her pulse jump as his fingers brushed her skin; felt her senses spring to life as she smelled his oh-so-familiar earthy male scent. How she'd missed him. Now that he was home, all she could think of was her aching desire to be in his arms.

"There," he said, when he finally clicked the tiny fastener in place. "That's it."

About to turn, she felt his hands curve around her upper arms, felt his chin rough on the top knob of her spine as he brushed a slow kiss over her neck.

"I've missed you." His voice was husky. "If I could have," he said, turning her around to face him, "I'd have cut the trip short but since I was the one with the vehicle, I could hardly take off and leave the others stranded 'way up there in the wilds—'"

"Why, Matt!" Naomi's delighted voice came from the doorway. "I didn't know you were back!"

Liz's breath shivered out. She'd forgotten that Matt's mother was in the house. And Naomi's timing couldn't have been worse, she reflected, with a feeling of wrenching disappointment. Being in Matt's arms had been bliss. She'd wanted to stay there forever.

But minutes later, as Naomi bustled around in the kitchen making tea while Matt went upstairs to shower and shave, Liz came to her senses and realized that the interruption had been for the best.

Certainly she had missed Matt desperately, but that very fact should have alerted her earlier to the fact that she had let herself become dangerously used to having him around. She had come to depend on it.

She didn't want to depend on "it" or on him. She didn't want to count on anyone again. Any psychologist would have told her, she realized, that this need for independence probably stemmed from her having been abandoned in the past by those she'd looked to for support—first by her mother when she died; then by Matt; then by her father; and lastly by Colin.

But whatever the reason, she was absolutely determined never to ask for help or support from anyone.

Ever again.

"Matt, will you have a look at that?" Frannie's tone held a thread of disgust. "It's snowing!"

Matt had just come out to the foyer from his office. Frannie was over by the window, midmorning mug of coffee in one hand, her eyes fixed on the street.

He joined her. And saw fat white flakes floating down from a winter-gray sky.

"Well," he said, "it *is* November. What did you expect!"

"But it's only the first week, we don't usually get snow this early! And it's heavy, and it's lying! I guess—" she turned with a mischievous smile

"—you'll be closing the office early so I can get home safely?"

"Frannie," he retorted, "since you walk to work and live only three blocks from here I don't foresee any problem!" His gaze moved across the street to the Clinic entrance. "No sign of Liz yet?"

"Uh-uh."

He tapped his fingers impatiently against his thighs. "Her checkups don't generally take this long."

"Maybe the doc's busy with another patient."

"Maybe. At any rate, I don't want her driving herself home, the roads could be dicey. I'm going to go over there, catch her before she leaves. Hold the fort?"

"Sure."

Matt grabbed his leather jacket from the coat stand by the door and shrugging it on, he went out and crossed the street to the clinic.

Three patients sat in the waiting room; of Liz there was no sign.

He was about to ask Sandy if she'd already left, when the waiting room door opened and Liz appeared.

She looked dazed.

And when she saw him, she blinked. "Matt?"

"It's snowing," he said. "I'm going to drive you home, then I'll walk back to the office."

To his surprise, she just nodded.

"Is everything all right?" he asked.

"Oh." Her eyes had a blank look. "Yes, everything's fine. Just hang on till I make my next appointment."

"Give me your keys," he said. "I'll bring the car to the door."

She fumbled in her bag and gave him the key.

He brought her car around from the car park at the

back of the building, and as he put it in Park at the curb, she appeared at the clinic door.

He hurried out of the car to take her arm as she crossed the snow-coated sidewalk.

Once she was ensconced in the passenger seat, he took his own seat and started off along the street.

"Liz, what the heck's up? You were looking great this morning, now you look as if somebody had dropped a ton of cement on your head."

"Let's wait," she said, "till we get home."

He clamped his lips together to keep from pressing her with more questions. But his concern increased with every passing moment. What had she found out in the doctor's office? Because undoubtedly she had found out something. He could barely wait to find out what it was.

"Twins, Matt." Liz's eyes still had a disbelieving look. "Dr. Black heard two heartbeats today." She slumped back in her kitchen chair, and rested her hands on the big mound of her belly. "He says there are two babies in there!"

Matt's chair had been tilted back; now it clattered forward abruptly. "Sheesh!" He stared back at Liz as what she'd said fully sank in. "Twins! He's sure?"

"Absolutely."

"No wonder you're so huge!" Matt grinned. "And no wonder you've been waddling around lately with all the elegance of a duck-billed platypus!"

Liz looked at him indignantly. "You've been telling me for weeks that I look fabulous, that pregnancy suits me, that—"

"You do, and it does, but—" He couldn't suppress a chuckle. "Heck, Liz, you have to admit that you—"

"That I look like the side of a house." She crinkled her nose. "But maybe not for too much longer. Dr. Black said that since it's twins, I may not go to full-term. While I was in his office, he called the local hospital, let them know I might be coming in before my due date."

"What puzzles me," Matt said, "is why he didn't notice earlier that there were two in there!"

"It sometimes happens that only one heartbeat is detectable. I did have an ultrasound in New York but it showed only one sac—because of that, I didn't even mention to Dr. Black that twins ran in Colin's family. If I had, I'm sure he'd have scheduled another ultrasound at some time."

"So…how do you feel about it?"

"It hasn't really sunk in yet. But how could I not be thrilled?"

"Are you…worried, at all?"

"I'm in good hands, with Dr. Black."

But though she spoke confidently, Matt couldn't help noticing that a shadow had clouded her eyes, and he knew that she *was* worried.

He wanted to say to her, "I'm here for you, sweetheart." And he was. He would never let her down again. She could depend on him for love and support and anything else she needed.

But he knew that she had no faith in him, and he knew that she'd rather walk around the world barefoot than ask him for help. Or anything else. So he said nothing.

It snowed heavily all night and in the morning a hard frost set in and gripped everything with its hoary fingers.

The roads were hard packed and squeaked under tires; the countryside was a fairyland of sparkling white, glittering in a pale hard sun that greedily hugged its heat to itself.

It didn't snow again but the cold snap continued.

For Liz, time now passed slowly. Unable to walk outside because of the icy ground, she felt restless, and for exercise had to resort to waddling along the passages and around the foyer and through the rooms, feeling heavier and more ungainly with each day that elapsed.

Besides her frequent need to empty her bladder, she suffered from a constantly nagging backache.

Matt stuffed pillows behind her whenever she sat down. "Chapter Ten," he announced cheerfully. "Page 212."

She also suffered from heartburn.

Matt made her sip ice-cold milk after her food, and told her to eat little and often. "Chapter Eleven," he told her as he brought her a plate of orange segments. "Page 225."

She suffered from a throbbing ache between her legs when standing. She didn't mention that to Matt but in any case he came home with a footstool one afternoon and stuck it under her feet when she sat down.

"Chapter Twelve," he said. "Page 234."

And all the while, the air was filled with classical music.

"Chapter Thirteen, page 240," he'd explained, as he inserted the first of several Mozart CDs into his stereo system. "The babies can hear music, it soothes them."

The music soothed her, too...but did nothing to help

her sleep at night. The babies were Sumo wrestlers. She knew it.

It made Matt chuckle to see her maternity top move as fists and feet and knees jutted out. And she had to chuckle, too. Though often, unknown to him, she felt like weeping. Hormones, she guessed. But she couldn't help worrying.

On the first of December, the weather changed. It grew a little warmer...the snow started to melt.

By the next day, the roads were clear.

Liz had a longer than usual nap after lunch, but even so she felt draggy and weary. When Matt came home, he settled her by a roaring log fire in the sitting room and after putting on a Beethoven CD, he brought her a light dinner on a tray, and then carried through his own meal.

Later, after he'd seen to the dishes, he came back to the sitting room.

"What's the weather doing?" Liz asked.

"It's turned cold again. Forecast's for a chance of rain through the night. Pretty dismal out."

As he sat down, Liz noticed he winced and then pressed a hand to his side. Against his ribs.

"What's wrong?" she asked.

"It's nothing." He grasped the arms of his chair and instead of looking directly at her as he usually did when he talked to her, he stared into the fire, at the orange and purple flames leaping up the throat of the chimney.

"Do you have a pain in your side?"

He seemed not to hear her; or not to be listening to her. *"Matt?"*

He jerked his head up then and looked at her. His

eyes were shuttered. "It's nothing. Just an old boxing injury."

"From the time you...had the beating?"

"Yeah." His tone was dismissive.

She had long wondered who he'd fought with on that occasion—and what woman wouldn't have, she mused, knowing that two men had come to blows over her, like a couple of great stags battling over a coveted doe. So she decided she would ask him about it, one more time.

Tentatively she said, "Why won't you talk about—"

He shot up from his seat. "There are some things," he said harshly, "that a man doesn't want to remember. All right?"

Tears sprang to her eyes and she quickly slanted her head down so he wouldn't see their sparkle.

"I'm going out for a walk," he snapped. "I'll be back in an hour."

Liz nodded, but sat still till she heard the front door slam shut behind him.

She breathed out a sigh. Poor Matt. He was worried about her. She knew that that was the only reason he had talked to her so roughly. Still, it hurt.

Weary and weepy, she heaved herself from her chair, and made her way out to the hall, walking awkwardly because of an uncomfortably heavy downward pressure—it felt almost as if the babies were going to drop out at any moment!

She wrote a note to Matt and left it on the hall table: Gone To Bed—Sorry I Upset You

She went upstairs, soaked in a warm bath and got into bed. For a change, she fell asleep right away, and for a change, she was undisturbed by anxious dreams.

* * *

When she woke again, it was ten after three. The house was quiet. She didn't need to go to the bathroom...so she wondered what could have disturbed her.

But even as she lay there, staring into the black, she felt a tight coil of pain clutch the small of her back.

And she knew then what had awakened her: she was in labor.

She lay there, hardly breathing, as she took in the momentousness of what was happening to her.

Then, swallowing back the sudden panic that had lumped in her throat, she levered herself up to a sitting position, and switched on the bedside light.

The babies had decided to come early into this world.

And Dr. Black had warned her that when they did decide to come, they would probably come quickly.

So she'd better not sit around here shaking and quaking. She'd better get her act together and move!

The hospital was only three miles away. Even driving carefully, she would be there within fifteen minutes.

With excitement and anticipation making her giddy, she maneuvered her huge bulk off the bed and lumbered around the room, gathering up her clothes, getting herself dressed.

Then retrieving her small suitcase from the closet where she'd stored it after packing her hospital necessities a week before, she tiptoed downstairs and crept outside.

She walked over to the Porsche, thankful that the night was dry...but thankful, too, for her warm wool jacket, which she huddled into to protect herself from the Arctic wind.

As she started up the engine and headed off down the drive, she found herself smiling. And she felt a surge of *immense* satisfaction.

She was going to have her babies. And she was doing this on her own, she didn't need anyone's help; not Matt's, not anyone else's.

Independence, she mused with a shamelessly confident smirk, was the name of the game!

She was halfway to the hospital when it started to rain.

Heavy rain.

She switched on the windshield wipers. And frowned, confused, when after the first dozen or so swipes, the glass no longer cleared.

It took a full ten seconds before she realized that what was lashing down was no ordinary rain.

It was *freezing* rain.

Rain that had coated the windshield with ice, swiftly and with absolutely no warning. And it took her completely by surprise.

Panicking, she flicked on the windshield washer.

To no effect.

Her panic exploded as she realized she was driving blind.

Heart thudding out of control, she rammed her foot to the brake…a foolish, foolish move for the car went into a wild skid. And at that very moment, a wave of excruciating pain grabbed her around the middle.

She cried out. Cried out in terror.

And as her scream echoed back in her ears, the Porsche skated over the icy road, and over the verge, to land, with a sickening crash, against the trunk of a massive tree.

CHAPTER TWELVE

MATT might not have heard Liz's bedroom door open if he hadn't been lying awake, unable to sleep because of his niggling guilt. His nasty little outburst had brought tears to her eyes, and it pained him to know he had hurt her.

He'd wanted to apologize but by the time he'd returned from his walk she'd gone to bed. It had frustrated him to realize he'd have to wait till morning to say he was sorry.

So when he heard her door open, he decided he'd wait till she came back from the bathroom and then he'd go and talk to her, get it off his chest and his conscience.

When she hadn't returned after ten minutes, he got up to check that she was all right.

The bathroom was empty.

Her bedroom door was ajar and when he checked her room, he found the bed was empty.

Not particularly worried, he went downstairs, expecting to find her in the kitchen, perhaps drinking a mug of warm milk.

What he found was a note:

Have Gone To The Hospital. Babes Are On Their Way.

He stared at it, his mouth hanging open. She'd gone to the hospital? She was in labor...and she'd taken it

171

upon herself to get there on her own? He'd known she was independent, but this was ridiculous!

Not only was it ridiculous, he reflected as he tore back upstairs, but it was heartbreakingly disappointing. If even at this most traumatic time she was determined to ''go it alone,'' then it was plain she would *never* seek his help. He should face up to that stark reality and accept it. But dammit, he just couldn't; it was too hard!

He'd never dressed faster, and was out of the house within a couple of minutes. Then when he did go out, he almost went flying on his back for to his dismay the ground was like a skating rink.

What the heck had happened since his earlier walk?

When he got into the car, he discovered he couldn't see out the windshield for ice.

Freezing rain. That's what had happened.

But *when* had it happened? Before or after Liz had reached the hospital? He hurriedly scraped the ice off the windshield, and tried to keep his apprehension from taking over.

But as he jumped into the Taurus and drove it gingerly down the driveway, he felt a rush of panic, panic that increased as he turned onto the highway and the car almost went into a tailspin.

Slowing to a snail's pace, he continued on his way, cursing with frustration, aching to accelerate but not daring to; and then, when he had gone about a mile along the deserted country road, he heard from up ahead the sound of a car horn…a continuous blare…as if someone had their hand pressed hard to the horn and was keeping it there.

Was it a cry for help?

Breath catching in his throat, he peered desperately

through the windshield as he drew closer to the sound; and all the time he prayed aloud that Liz was all right.

Then as suddenly as it had started, the sound stopped.

He guided the car forward, inch by inch, all the while darting his gaze here, there, and everywhere, frantically trying to find the source of the now ominously silent horn.

And when he rounded a bend in the highway his worst fear became reality, for there, up ahead and starkly illuminated in the headlights of the Taurus, was the very thing he had most dreaded seeing: a car that had skidded off the road and had smashed, headfirst, into a tree.

And in his soul he knew, even before he was close enough to recognize it, that the vehicle was a midnight blue Porsche.

Liz fought to survive yet another wave of pain.

It had come so fast after the last, it had sent her fear spiraling to an even higher level. And when it finally passed, leaving her limp and exhausted, she pulled open her coat and desperately ran searching palms over her belly, praying to feel the impatient jut of an elbow, the aggressive thrust of a foot.

Nothing.

Despair threatened to overwhelm her.

Even if she could have managed to get the car door open—which she couldn't—she knew that trying to walk to the hospital would be unthinkable. She'd never make it. She'd lose her balance on the icy road before she'd taken two steps.

Her only hope was that someone would drive past, hear her horn, see her car. Save her babies.

She pressed her hand to the horn again and kept it there, until another wave of pain hit her, making her cry out. She tried to relax, to ride with the contraction, but she'd never known anything like it. Dear God, she prayed, please help me. I should have asked Matt to drive me, I shouldn't have been so independent, if only, if only—

Someone wrenched open her car door. Gasping, she jerked her head around and winced as the white beam of a flashlight dazzled her eyes, blinding her.

"Help me," she cried. "Oh, please help—"

"Damned right I'll help you." Matt's voice was grim but it shook with emotion; and it was the sweetest sound she had ever heard. "Hang in there, sweetheart. I promise you I'll get you to the hospital in time."

He did.

But afterward he swore that an angel must have taken over and driven his car over the ice-glazed roads for him, because he had no recollection of anything other than talking quietly to Liz, trying to reassure her, while she struggled to cope with contractions that were getting closer and closer together.

When finally he saw the lights of the hospital's Emergency Entrance ahead, he said, with enormous relief, "We're here, sweetheart. We've made it!"

Her response was a groan so agonized it made him want to weep.

But this was not the moment to offer comfort. He braked to a halt under the wide-canopied entrance doors and with a breathless, "Be right back!" shot into the building.

Within thirty seconds he was striding back out

again, accompanied by two hurrying attendants with a wheelchair.

And from then on in, it was out of his hands. He had done all he could for the woman he loved.

Now all he could do was wait.

And pray.

"You did well, Liz." Dr. Black stood at Liz's bedside, and smiled down at her. "Your babies are truly beautiful."

"They are, aren't they! And...you said they were healthy?" Liz asked anxiously.

He laughed. "How often do you have to hear it? They're just great."

"I know...it's just...it's so hard to take it all in." Liz threaded back her hair and felt it damp with perspiration. But though the delivery had been the hardest work she'd ever done, and her body felt as if it had been run through a wringer, her soul was soaring, powered by joy.

She saw the doctor yawn, and she said wryly, "I'm sorry I had to get you out of bed in the middle of the night!"

"Hey, delivering babies is one of the neatest perks of this job. But I'm going home now—my wife'll have my breakfast waiting! Before I go, though...there's a young man outside who's waiting to see you."

"Matt? He's still here?"

"Are you kidding? If I didn't know better, I'd think he was the new dad! He's been standing outside the nursery, gawking through the glass at those infants with as much awe and reverence as if they were his own!"

Liz felt her heart give an odd twist as she pictured him looking at the babies.

"It's thanks to Matt," she murmured, "that the babies and I got here safely. I owe him...everything."

"Why don't you tell him? I want you to rest, Liz, but he can visit for a couple of minutes."

As the door swung shut behind the doctor, Liz closed her eyes and set a hand gently on her stomach. It felt flat under the light cover. Amazing. Wonderful. After all those months of being big as an elephant, so ungainly, so—

"Hi."

Her eyes flew open at the sound of Matt's voice.

He was standing in the doorway, hesitantly. His navy sweatshirt, she noticed, was back to front; he must have dressed in a hurry. And his hair was tousled, his jaw unshaven. "Matt," she whispered. "Hi."

He walked slowly over to the bed. She'd never seen him look so serious, yet at the same time, his eyes were alight with wonder.

"You've seen the babies?" she asked softly.

"Yeah." A grin creased his face, banished the seriousness. "A boy and a girl. What could be nicer?"

"You didn't have to stay, Matt, after you drove me here, it's been *hours*—"

"Where else would I be?" He dragged a chair over and sitting down by the bed, took her hands in his. "Where else would I *want* to be! Sweetheart, we've been living together for the past months, I've watched those babies grow, I feel...*involved* with them. As involved as if they were my own. Liz, they're beautiful. So blond, so sweet. I'd never seen babies so new before, and they're so tiny." Tears came to his eyes. "It makes me blubber, just thinking of them."

Liz felt her own eyes fill up. "Matt, how can I ever thank you for getting me here? How did you know I'd gone out? I tried to be so quiet, I wanted to get here on my own, but—"

"I have *never* known such an independent woman!"

"I was wrong, Matt. I know that now. I endangered the lives of my babies with my stubborn insistence on being independent. I thought I could do everything by myself, but when it came to the crunch I *did* need help. I ended up *begging* for it. And you—instead of saying, 'I told you so!' you couldn't have been kinder." Her voice cracked. But she managed to go on, and say what had to be said. "I'm ashamed of myself, Matt, for the way I've been to you since I came back home. Can you ever forgive me? I know it's—"

"I love you, Liz."

He hadn't even been listening to her; she could see that now. His eyes were dark with intensity; fixed on her with an expression that made her feel giddy.

"Liz, I've never loved anyone but you. And I never will. I'm a one-woman man, always have been, always will be. If you weren't so exhausted and vulnerable, I would get down on my knees by this bed and ask you to marry me. Besides, the doc gave me only a minute. But I'll be back. Later on today. And I'll be asking you that question then. Please try to have the right answer ready."

And then, with a heart-melting smile, and a farewell salute, he was gone.

"You have a visitor waiting," the nurse said as she plumped Liz's pillows. "Naomi Garvock. I've told her she'll have to be patient, visiting hours don't start till two...but she's quite happy, looking at the twins, in the nursery.''

Liz was glad her visitor was Naomi, and not Matt. Her mind had been in a turmoil ever since his promise to propose. She still couldn't decide how to answer him. She loved him, with all her heart. And what he had done for her last night had more than made up for his lack of support thirteen years ago. But...it still niggled that while she'd suffered alone through such a heartbreaking loss, he'd got off scot-free. What if they were to marry, and then one day they fought— as most married couples do!—and what if she were to cast it up, throw it in his face, let him know that the bitterness of it still ate at her—

''I haven't seen Naomi Garvock in here for years.'' The nurse popped a thermometer into Liz's mouth. ''Not since the time her boy was brought in...so bruised and battered and broken he was unrecognizable...and he was in here for *weeks*. We all said that whoever beat him up that night should have been thrown in jail, but...Matt would never say who did it.''

The door swung open and Naomi appeared. She was carrying a pot of cream chrysanthemums. ''Two o'clock, nurse,'' she said. ''Okay if I come in now?''

''Sure.''

Beaming, Naomi crossed to the bed, and gave Liz a kiss. ''Honey, I'm so thrilled that everything went well, Matt called me this morning, first thing, and told me the whole story. The babies are glorious,'' she babbled on happily. ''Absolutely adorable. By the way, Matt's gone to Crestville—he had some errands to run—but he told me to let you know he'll visit this evening.''

The nurse removed the thermometer. "I was just saying to this young lady that I hadn't seen you nor your boy in here since the time he was beaten up." She checked the thermometer reading, gave a satisfied nod. "Never did find out who did it, did they?" She flicked Naomi an inquisitive glance.

"No," Naomi said firmly, "they did not."

"Ah well…" With a vague smile to Liz, the nurse went out.

"Oh!" Naomi rolled her eyes. "That one is such a gossip! Be careful what you say to her or it'll be all over town before you know it!" She crossed to the windowsill, and moved things around to find the best spot for her potted plant. "Matt never wanted anyone to find out," she added over her shoulder, "that your father was the one who almost killed him. He knew that if it got out, people would conclude that there could be only one reason why Max Rossiter would go after him, and since no one else had been aware of your pregnancy, he wanted to keep it that way to protect your reputation so—"

"My *father?*" Feeling sick with disbelief, Liz stared at Naomi. "My *father* was the one who—"

"Oh, dear." Naomi turned around, and her expression was vexed. "You didn't know? You and Matt have become so close, I just assumed that by now he would have told you—I mean, you must have asked how he got his nose broken and—"

"I did ask." Liz strove to come to grips with what she'd just learned. "But he wouldn't tell me." She pushed herself up on one elbow and said weakly, "Naomi, what happened? Please, I need to know. He was my father, I need to know how he could have done such a terrible thing. Oh, I realize the reason—he must

have somehow found out Matt was my baby's father—
but Matt could have outboxed my father with one hand
tied around his back!''

''Matt didn't fight.''

Blankly Liz gazed at her. ''Pardon?''

''Matt didn't fight.''

Liz stared numbly. ''I don't understand…''

''Your father did find out, Liz, that Matt was the
baby's father—he'd heard Matt had been asking questions in town, asking people if they knew where you
were.'' Naomi bit her lip, and then said, ''I'm going
to tell you what happened, because I think you ought
to know…although Matt will be angry with me when
he finds out.'' She glanced warily at the door as footsteps passed by, and then lowering her voice, she said,
''Do you remember telling me you considered Matt
got off scot-free?''

Liz nodded. ''And you…wanted to tell me something, but stopped yourself. Was it…about Matt and
my father?''

''Your father came hammering on our door one
night, very late. Matt and I…we both heard him, got
up, came downstairs together, looked out the window.
And when we saw who it was, Matt said, 'He's looking for me.' He sounded hard and grim. He grabbed
my shoulders and looked me straight in the eye and
said, in a voice I'd never heard him use before: 'Whatever happens out there, I want you to stay inside. And
do nothing. *Promise me that.*' ''

''Did *you* know why my father was there?''

''Not until afterward. Liz, Matt didn't defend himself. Your father…well, you know what a big brute of
a man he was. But Matt just stood there…like some
sacrifice. As if he was doing penance.'' Naomi

brushed a hand over her eyes. "I stayed inside, as he'd wanted me to, until...after it was all over and your father had gone, leaving Matt alone...and unconscious...on the sidewalk."

Liz realized tears were pouring down her cheeks, she felt their warm salty taste at the corners of her mouth. She also felt as if her heart was breaking. "He could have danced rings around my father," she whispered.

"I know," Naomi said sadly. "Darling, I know. But he knew he'd done something wrong and he wanted to pay the price."

Matt had never felt so nervous in his life.

As he walked along the corridor toward the maternity wing, he clutched the bouquet of yellow roses so tightly he felt the thorns stab his flesh. Damn. He slackened his grip.

He'd thought of buying red, for true love, but he knew yellow was Liz's favorite color.

He also knew that amethysts were her favorite gemstone, so the ring he'd bought that afternoon in Crestville—before he'd visited the bookstore in search of the book he'd wanted!—was an amethyst set in platinum.

Now all he had to do was convince her to accept it.

He was glad she was in a private room, he didn't want anyone around when he asked the question.

But when he walked into her room he discovered there *were* going to be people around when he asked the question. Two very small people, who were at present nestled in the arms of their radiant mom. Two tiny babes, one in pink, the other in blue—and both of them mind-blowingly adorable.

And Liz herself, though she looked pale and her flaxen hair was limp and she was wearing only a simple leaf-green hospital gown, was to him the most beautiful sight in the world.

He cleared his throat.

"I brought you some flowers," he said. "Where do they go?"

"You'll find a vase over there." She pointed to a glass vase by the sink. "They're lovely, Matt. Thank you."

He stuck the roses into the vase with some water and set it on the windowsill next a pot of cream 'mums.

"Pull over a chair," Liz said. "And come say 'Hi' to these two little angels."

They were sound asleep. As he sat down, all he could see of them were pink faces, dainty noses, wisps of hair a shade or two lighter than their mother's. He leaned over, and brushed a kiss over each smooth brow. They smelled milky sweet. The baby in blue blew out a frothy bubble; the other stuck a fist into her mouth and started to gum it.

Matt gazed at them fondly for a long time. And then he turned his attention to Liz.

"How are you feeling?" he asked. "Everything okay?"

"I feel wonderful," she said. "Just great. It's such a huge relief to have it all over safely, to have two such perfect little babies!"

"Have you decided what you're going to call them?"

Her eyes were dreamy. "I'd like to call the little girl Naomi Jane. Jane was my mom's name," she explained. "And I've grown so fond of Naomi."

"She'll be honored," Matt said. And he knew she would. "How about the little guy?"

"Well, this is really difficult." Liz crinkled her nose in that delightful way she had. "You see, I'd like to name him after the man who'll be helping me bring him up, only...I have to ask him first how he'd feel about that."

Matt blinked. This man was going to *help* her bring up her babies? But Liz Rossiter...the new Liz Rossiter, the one who had arrived from New York with the light of battle in her eyes...had intended to bring up her babies alone. She had made that quite clear.

Unless...

He tried to fight a growing feeling of apprehension. "Have you...you haven't been in touch with...that guy in New York...have you?"

She *tutted*. And with lips twitching, looked down at her sleeping babes. She kissed one and then the other before addressing them in a soft voice.

"You don't *really* want this man for your dad, do you? He seems awfully thick...and that may be all right in a father, but in a husband...well, the way I see it, intelligence should be right up there as a non-negotiable quality, along with a sense of humor, a sense of responsibility, a—"

"Lizbeth Rossiter." Matt could hardly speak for the sheer exultation soaring up inside him. "You're talking about *me?* Does that mean...is this a *yes?*"

She kept him in suspense for a full ten seconds. And then she nodded. Her eyes were shining.

He couldn't speak for a few moments, such was his joy. When finally he got his act together, he said gruffly, "You're bold as brass, woman! You might at least have had the decency to wait till you were asked!''

He went down on his knees. "Liz, my dearest precious Liz, I love you with all my heart, now and forever more, so will you please put me out of my misery and marry me!''

"My answer,'' she said primly, "is exactly the same as it was a moment ago!''

"And that's your *final* answer?''

Laughter bubbled from her; music to his ears.

He kissed her then, and she returned his kiss with such uninhibited passion that if she hadn't been encumbered by the twins, he'd have climbed right into bed with her.

Instead he brought out the ring and slipped it on her finger.

"Oh, Matt.'' She gazed at it mistily. "It's perfect.''

They kissed again, slowly this time, sweetly, with the promise of thousands of tomorrows lying shimmering ahead.

After a while, Matt said, "Liz, about the house—''

Her eyes told him that ownership of her former home was something that no longer needed to be discussed. Laurel House wasn't going to be his; it wasn't going to be hers; it was going to be theirs. "Why did you buy it, Matt? I know it had to be something more than just its proximity to town and the wonderful view…''

"Yeah,'' he said. "It was something more. I didn't admit it to myself at the time, but I know now that in my heart of hearts, I dreamed that one day you'd come home again, I dreamed that the past would be forgiven and forgotten and…we'd be together again.''

Liz framed his rugged face with her hands, and

gently kissed his flat cheek; his broken nose; his scarred lip.

"Your mother," she whispered, "told me how you received your scars, Matt. I'm so sorry."

His breath caught sharply. And then he felt the quick tension ease. It was just as well Liz knew; he didn't want there to be any more secrets between them. Ever.

"Don't be, my darling. It's over. The past is over."

Tears sparkled like silver sequins in her beautiful eyes. "Yes," she agreed huskily. "It is finally over."

"And the future is right here, in your arms."

As if the babes sensed they were being spoken about, they stirred, and squinted hazily up at their mom.

"Look, Matt," Liz said excitedly. "They're *smiling!*"

"Uh-uh." He shook his head. "It's just wind."

"Really?" She stared at him, surprised. "How do you know?"

He took her left hand and ran a fingertip lovingly over the amethyst engagement ring that proclaimed her his own.

"Chapter One," he explained smugly, "page 17, the *Handy Hardback Guide For Brand-New Parents Of Twins.*"

PARENTS WANTED

Families in the making!

In the orphanage of a small Australian town called Bay Beach are little children desperately in need of love, and dreaming of their very own family....

The answer to their dreams can also be found in Bay Beach! Couples who are destined for each other—even if they don't know it yet. Brought together by love for these tiny children, can they find true love themselves—and finally become a real family?

Titles in this series by fan-favorite **MARION LENNOX** are

A Child in Need—(April HR #3650)
Their Baby Bargain—(July HR #3662)

Look out for further Parents Wanted stories in Harlequin Romance®, coming soon!

Available wherever Harlequin Books are sold.

HARLEQUIN®
Makes any time special ®

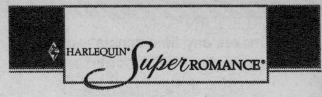

HARLEQUIN *Super* ROMANCE®

**To celebrate the
1000th Superromance book
We're presenting you with 3 books
from 3 of your favorite authors in**

All Summer Long

Home, Hearth and Haley
by **Muriel Jensen**

Meet the men and women of Muriel's
upcoming **Men of Maple Hill** trilogy

Daddy's Girl
by **Judith Arnold**

Another **Daddy School** story!

Temperature Rising
by **Bobby Hutchinson**

Life and love at St. Joe's Hospital are as feverish
as ever in this **Emergency!** story

On sale July 2001
Available wherever Harlequin books are sold.

HARLEQUIN®
Makes any time special ®

Double your pleasure—
with this collection containing two full-length

Harlequin Romance®

novels

New York Times bestselling author

DEBBIE MACOMBER

delivers

RAINY DAY KISSES

While Susannah Simmons struggles up the corporate
ladder, her neighbor Nate Townsend stays home baking
cookies and flying kites. She resents the way he questions
her values—and the way he messes up her five-year plan
when she falls in love with him!

PLUS

THE BRIDE PRICE

a brand-new novel by reader favorite

DAY LECLAIRE

On sale July 2001

HARLEQUIN®

Makes any time special®

Harlequin truly does make any time special. . . . This year we are celebrating weddings in style!

A Walk Down the Aisle

WEDDING CELEBRATION

To help us celebrate, we want you to tell us how wearing the Harlequin wedding gown will make your wedding day special. As the grand prize, Harlequin will offer one lucky bride the chance to **"Walk Down the Aisle"** in the Harlequin wedding gown!

There's more...

For her honeymoon, she and her groom will spend five nights at the **Hyatt Regency Maui.** As part of this five-night honeymoon at the hotel renowned for its romantic attractions, the couple will enjoy a candlelit dinner for two in Swan Court, a sunset sail on the hotel's catamaran, and duet spa treatments.

A HYATT RESORT AND SPA®   Maui • Molokai • Lanai

To enter, please write, in, 250 words or less, how wearing the Harlequin wedding gown will make your wedding day special. The entry will be judged based on its emotionally compelling nature, its originality and creativity, and its sincerity. This contest is open to Canadian and U.S. residents only and to those who are 18 years of age and older. There is no purchase necessary to enter. Void where prohibited. See further contest rules attached. Please send your entry to:

Walk Down the Aisle Contest

In Canada
P.O. Box 637
Fort Erie, Ontario
L2A 5X3

In U.S.A.
P.O. Box 9076
3010 Walden Ave.
Buffalo, NY 14269-9076

You can also enter by visiting www.eHarlequin.com
Win the Harlequin wedding gown and the vacation of a lifetime!
The deadline for entries is October 1, 2001.

HARLEQUIN®
Makes any time special ®

PHWDACONT1

1. To enter, follow directions published in the offer to which you are responding. Contest begins April 2, 2001, and ends on October 1, 2001. Method of entry may vary. Mailed entries must be postmarked by October 1, 2001, and received by October 8, 2001.

2. Contest entry may be, at times, presented via the Internet, but will be restricted solely to residents of certain geographic areas that are disclosed on the Web site. To enter via the Internet, if permissible, access the Harlequin Web site (www.eHarlequin.com) and follow the directions displayed online. Online entries must be received by 11:59 p.m. E.S.T. on October 1, 2001.

   In lieu of submitting an entry online, enter by mail by hand-printing (or typing) on an 8½" x 11" plain piece of paper, your name, address (including zip code), Contest number/name and in 250 words or fewer, why winning a Harlequin wedding c would make your wedding day special. Mail via first-class mail to: Harlequin Walk Down the Aisle Contest 1197, (in the U P.O. Box 9076, 3010 Walden Avenue, Buffalo, NY 14269-9076, (in Canada) P.O. Box 637, Fort Erie, Ontario L2A 5X3, Can

   Limit one entry per person, household address and e-mail address. Online and/or mailed entries received from persons residing in geographic areas in which Internet entry is not permissible will be disqualified.

3. Contests will be judged by a panel of members of the Harlequin editorial, marketing and public relations staff based on the following criteria:

   - Originality and Creativity—50%
   - Emotionally Compelling—25%
   - Sincerity—25%

   In the event of a tie, duplicate prizes will be awarded. Decisions of the judges are final.

4. All entries become the property of Torstar Corp. and will not be returned. No responsibility is assumed for lost, late, illegit incomplete, inaccurate, nondelivered or misdirected mail or misdirected e-mail, for technical, hardware or software failures any kind, lost or unavailable network connections, or failed, incomplete, garbled or delayed computer transmission or any human error which may occur in the receipt or processing of the entries in this Contest.

5. Contest open only to residents of the U.S. (except Puerto Rico) and Canada, who are 18 years of age or older, and is void wherever prohibited by law; all applicable laws and regulations apply. Any litigation within the Province of Quebec respectir the conduct or organization of a publicity contest may be submitted to the Régie des alcools, des courses et des jeux for a ruling. Any litigation respecting the awarding of a prize may be submitted to the Régie des alcools, des courses et des jeu for the purpose of helping the parties reach a settlement. Employees and immediate family members of Torstar Corp. and D. L. Blair, Inc., their affiliates, subsidiaries and all other agencies, entities and persons connected with the use, marketing conduct of this Contest are not eligible to enter. Taxes on prizes are the sole responsibility of winners. Acceptance of any p offered constitutes permission to use winner's name, photograph or other likeness for the purposes of advertising, trade ar promotion on behalf of Torstar Corp., its affiliates and subsidiaries without further compensation to the winner, unless prohibited by law.

6. Winners will be determined no later than November 15, 2001, and will be notified by mail. Winners will be required to sigr return an Affidavit of Eligibility form within 15 days after winner notification. Noncompliance within that time period may re in disqualification and an alternative winner may be selected. Winners of trip must execute a Release of Liability prior to tic and must possess required travel documents (e.g. passport, photo ID) where applicable. Trip must be completed by Noven 2002. No substitution of prize permitted by winner. Torstar Corp. and D. L. Blair, Inc., their parents, affiliates, and subsidiar are not responsible for errors in printing or electronic presentation of Contest, entries and/or game pieces. In the event of printing or other errors which may result in unintended prize values or duplication of prizes, all affected game pieces or en shall be null and void. If for any reason the Internet portion of the Contest is not capable of running as planned, including infection by computer virus, bugs, tampering, unauthorized intervention, fraud, technical failures, or any other causes beyc the control of Torstar Corp. which corrupt or affect the administration, secrecy, fairness, integrity or proper conduct of the Contest, Torstar Corp. reserves the right, at its sole discretion, to disqualify any individual who tampers with the entry proc and to cancel, terminate, modify or suspend the Contest or the Internet portion thereof. In the event of a dispute regarding online entry, the entry will be deemed submitted by the authorized holder of the e-mail account submitted at the time of ent Authorized account holder is defined as the natural person who is assigned to an e-mail address by an Internet access pro online service provider or other organization that is responsible for arranging e-mail address for the domain associated wi submitted e-mail address. **Purchase or acceptance of a product offer does not improve your chances of winn**

7. Prizes: (1) Grand Prize—A Harlequin wedding dress (approximate retail value: $3,500) and a 5-night/6-day honeymoon t Maui, HI, including round-trip air transportation provided by Maui Visitors Bureau from Los Angeles International Airport (winner is responsible for transportation to and from Los Angeles International Airport) and a Harlequin Romance Packag including hotel accomodations (double occupancy) at the Hyatt Regency Maui Resort and Spa, dinner for (2) two at Swar Court, a sunset sail on Kiele V and a spa treatment for the winner (approximate retail value: $4,000); (5) Five runner-up p of a $1000 gift certificate to selected retail outlets to be determined by Sponsor (retail value $1000 ea.). Prizes consist of those items listed as part of the prize. Limit one prize per person. All prizes are valued in U.S. currency.

8. For a list of winners (available after December 17, 2001) send a self-addressed, stamped envelope to: Harlequin Walk Do Aisle Contest 1197 Winners, P.O. Box 4200 Blair, NE 68009-4200 or you may access the www.eHarlequin.com Web site through January 15, 2002.

Contest sponsored by Torstar Corp., P.O. Box 9042, Buffalo, NY 14269-9042, U.S.A.